MW00942373

bite size reads

slightly twisted, deliciously dark,
really short stories for people with very little time
or very short attention spans

by

R B Frank

Cover and interiors: R.Frank with MariaLoren Designs

ISBN-13: 978-1532820397
ISBN-10: 1532820399

Wait! Before you start…

Bite Size Reads is divided into three sections to help you choose what you want to read depending on how much time you have. What's so cool about this collection is that each story has an **Average Read Time.** Just guesstimate how much time you have and pick a story within that section.

You've got:

Morsels are 4 minutes or less.
Tidbits are between 5 and 10 minutes.
Cup o' Joe Stories are between 1 and 15 minutes, and are fully satisfying.

So, do you have time for coffee, a Tidbit or just a Morsel?

"Yeah, but when do I have time to read?"

Here are some ideas:

Your teacher is late
Your boss is late
Everyone is late – always
Your Starbucks is not ready
Your pizza is not ready
The copy machine is jammed
On line at the bank
On line at the Post Office
On line at Target
(because you'll be there FOREVER)
At the doctor's
(because you'll be there FOREVER)

At those excruciatingly long traffic lights
On the bus
Waiting for the bus
On the subway
Waiting for the subway
On the toilet
Waiting for help at an unnamed self-improvement store
On line at school pick-up
At one of my book signings

You get the idea. So get off social media and feed your mind with twisted tales of fate, creepy morsels and delicious turns of irony. And sprinkled in almost all of them is a bit of humor.

And remember, a good read can happen one bite at a time.

Enjoy!

R.B. Frank - May 2016

Table of Contents

Morsels
Average Read Time less than 4 Minutes

Tidbits
Average Read Time between 5 and 10 Minutes

Cup o' Joe Stories

For those quieter moments.

After Dinner Mints

Morsels

Expectations and Misunderstandings

Average Read Time: 1 ½ min.

Today's the day. That's what Heather heard from Cecilia, who heard it from Rona, who heard it from Isabelle, who is dating Pete, Jeremy's best bud.

Pete told Isabelle, "Yeah, all Jeremy talks about is Heather and that TODAY will be The Day."

So at 6:00 that evening, Jeremy surprised her with a trip to Wo Hop's in Chinatown, the memorable but hole-in-the-wall place of their first date, and she waited patiently through a serving of dumplings, greasy Lo Mein and Lemon Chicken.

A box with a shiny ring did not appear.

Heather excused herself from the table to "go whiz," as she calls it. She texted Cecilia: "No ring. R u sure?"

1

"That's what Rona told me. Pete said Jeremy said today's the day."

"Jeremy's screwing up again." Maybe he has a carriage ride or something planned afterwards.

Heather returned to the table and finished her chicken.

Jeremy watched her shovel the last of the rice on her fork. "Heather, I have something to say."

Oh, goody.

"I know what you were doing while I was in Iraq. With Pete and Jason. And your little walk on the wild side with Crackhead Peggy from the 7-11."

Hm. Not what she expected.

He held her hand across the fortune cookies. Again, not what she expected.

"I sprinkled your chicken with tetrodotoxin." He smiled at her furrowed brow. "That's Pufferfish venom, easily acquired in Chinatown, by the way."

Yeah, really, really not what she expected. At all. And Heather's extremities numbed quickly as Jeremy's face morphed into a Picasso painting.

Skin Deep

Average Read Time: 3 min

"Doc, don't you see it? All there, under there," I said pointing to my arm.

"There's nothing there, Mr. Puckett, I assure you." The doctor didn't see anything. They always say that. Every one of them.

Bugs never bothered me before, but when my dog got fleas, I had to fumigate my house. They didn't get all of them. Missed some. The left-overs nested in my hair. I could tell by the itch. I itched like a dog. The itching was insane.

Then there were others. Other bugs joined in. On me. In me.

I was like an open house to the insect world. Thousands of spider-like arachnids scurried up my leg, my body and, at times, they coated the back of my neck. They got into my hair, spinning their webs on the follicles. Sticky, gummy strings glued to my scalp. See

3

them? Go ahead. Look. There. The black crawly things have legs and antenna.

My regular doctor couldn't see anything, so he referred me to a dermatologist who couldn't see the bugs on me or under my skin. After that, I made my rounds to every "ologist" out there. Some you wouldn't even think should see regular people. Scientists. Not doctor-doctors. I went to an entomologist at the University of Scranton who couldn't see any of the creepy crawlies feasting on my epidermis. He said, "I don't see anything, Mr. Puckett, but I have a friend." The friend was a last ditch effort to get answers and I travelled to see a…parasitologist in the city as there aren't many (any) parasitologists in the Poconos. They specialize in bugs who burrow in the skin and lay their eggs.

I thought, *Bingo.* That's what's happening, you know. Squirming and laying their eggs. Making more. Just below the surface, you can just make out their coiled up worm like shape, wiggling. Spreading under my skin. I can feel them invading. Sometimes I scratch until my skin bleeds. Those scars; that's where I let them out.

I wasn't sure what they were so I did what every other person would do. Consulted the internet. And in 0.701 blah-blah-blah seconds I found they're called nematodes. The name is just as disgusting as the critter. Mini eels moving around under my skin.

So the parasite doctor agreed to see me as I told him I had nematodes and crawling critters. He said the possibility of harboring bugs under the skin was highly unlikely, unless I had been to Guatemala. I had not.

But I had spiders. And fleas. And nematodes. And this could make him famous in all the scientific journals. A genius among his peers. His legacy immortalized in the headlines of the National Enquirer:

*"Man in Poconos Infested with Skin
Burrowing Bugs -Man Describes
Harrowing Experience.*

NYC Parasitologist a Hero."

He saw nothing.

He took skin samples right where I told him. He viewed them under his electron microscope. "There are no parasites, Mr. Puckett, which I can see." And then after a pause, he suggested one more "ologist." A psychologist.

I don't need a psychologist. They're there. The million legs crawling in my hair, in my ears. The ones squirming, there, on my arm. Another group of the buggers are in my thigh, making their way up my leg…uh…to my stomach. They're moving. Always moving. And the crawly ones, if I scratch, they scatter. God, the itch. It's worse at night. They're more active at night. Nocturnal creatures.

I don't need another doctor to tell me they're not there. Come closer, I'll show you the worms. I watched how the doctor took a skin sample. Oh, don't worry. I sterilized this. I had this X-Acto knife from art class. Let me peel just a thin layer. You pull it with the tweezers. Careful. See them?

Oh, God. Say you see them.

Anywhere But Here

Average Read Time: 1 ½ min

My wife Meg never shops. She hunts. So when she announces that she wants a new sofa, I put on my weekend basketball sneaks and eat a solid breakfast. I load the girls up with protein so their little bodies, at five and three, won't fail them.

We head for the Furniture Warehouse Outlet, which is aptly named because it's an outlet in a once-upon-a-time factory warehouse. Which also means miles and miles of sofas. She enters with clear determination and focus. The girls follow behind like ducklings in a pond. Quack, quack, quack, quack. The smallest clings to the back of her sister's shirt for fear of being left behind as her mother navigates the maze with lightning speed. Every so often, the older one swats behind her because that's gotta be annoying. I tag behind them, giving my mid-age arthritic feet a workout.

7

Meg weaves in and out and around pretend living rooms, her eyes darting left and right with laser precision. I'm already huffing and puffing. Asking her to slow down would be like trying to quell the frenetic energy of electrons around an atom.

A pleasantly plump salesperson sees Meg frowning and she asks, "Can I help you find something?" *She doesn't know what she's in for.*

Meg answers, "I just want a slipcover sofa. How hard is it to find that?"

Victim Number One looks as if her feelings were just hurt and says, "Let's see what we can find, then." And we shift into third gear once again.

We skirt by sofa after sofa. *Pick one already!* The girls giggle behind her, oblivious to the fluid motion of stress their mother leaves in her wake.

"Meg. How 'bout this one?"

"No. Too transitional."

What the hell is that?

Then I hear, "Yeah, Dad. Too tramstitchable." *Press One. Copy.*

More and more behemoths wiz by my field of vision. The sofas all begin to look the same to me, but I hear authoritative comments like "stunning French curves" and about "being enveloped in luxurious fabrics."

It's furniture porn.

Two hours later, Meg has alienated three sales people and the girls have gone through two juice boxes and a bag of popcorn. I flop in an over-sized leather recliner and watch a pretend Giants game on a pretend big screen. I hear Meg's voice echo off the exposed warehouse ceiling. I have no idea where the girls are anymore.

I close my eyes and drift away. The turmoil that is Meg, fades.

I take out my phone and check the time. Exactly eight hours and thirty five minutes until —

When I am with Andrea, it's just so…quiet.

The Last Wine Cooler
on the
Fourth of July

Average Read Time: 2 min

Cheryl stroked her pinky on Todd's hand. "Another wine cooler?'

"Sure."

She lifted her bulbous torso from the lawn chair and Todd pinched her butt as she passed. Cheryl made an attempt to swipe his hand. Attempt, mind you.

She opened the top of the cooler. There were none left. She sneered at Steven, the one she considered her real significant other because she called his trailer home.

She turned to Carl, mutual friend of Todd and Steven, and Cheryl's other part-time diversion. "Carl, can you believe Steven only packed two wine coolers? Who packs only two wine coolers?"

Steven looked up, but was very intent on setting up the bottle rockets in the clearing.

Carl chipped the remaining two golf balls into the sump then he settled into his folding sports chair.

Cheryl called across the clearing, "Steven, I told you to bring all of the wine coolers!" Her massive body and energy approached Steven just as he finished placing the fireworks in the empty beer bottles. "Did you hear me?"

Steven ignored her noise.

Cheryl waddled back over to Carl and sat on his lap, with a little extra grind. "Now I have to go back to the house and get more," she pouted, "because who wants to drink the cheap crap beer that's left?"

Carl slipped his hand between her sausage stuffed Jeggings. Todd winked at Carl, knowing what was to come.

"I'll be back," she said. She threw a nasty look at Steven. "Stupid ass."

Cheryl's buffalo-back made a perfect target. Todd and Carl joined Steven in the clearing and each took a bottle. Each lit his own bottle rocket and aimed it at the NASCAR emblem on the back of her shirt. Sparks, clothing and flesh rained over the clearing. They couldn't tell if the screeching was Cheryl or the fireworks.

"Tragic accident," said Steven.

"Tragic," said Carl as he handed Steven and Todd a golf club. "We said when we were six that nothing would come between The Three Musketeers."

They lifted their Big Berthas and made the iconic triangle in the acrid, hanging smoke.

Steven smiled, "One for all —"

"And all for one," his buddies finished. They shoved their clubs into the divots and leaned on their clubs.

"Who's going to call 911?" said Steven.

"I'll do it. I did some acting in school," said Todd. "Tee time is 8:15 tomorrow."

"You think we'll make it?" asked Steven.

"Ah, plenty of time," said Carl.

Halloween 2.0

Average Read Time: 3 min 25 sec.

Robert pressed the button of his digital recorder.

"New World Podcast, number one. October 31st." He shook his head and cleared his throat. "Happy Halloween, my new listeners. I started this podcast to let others know you can survive. We are here. And you can find us.

The calendar says twelve months to the date since the first outbreak of the virus. Seems like forever ago. I didn't understand how big this thing was at the beginning. I'm sure you didn't either. Life imitating art…or our nightmares, right? My wife and I knew right away we needed to leave. We moved our family to our cabin until things settled down. My youngest whined about leaving but we couldn't have our kids listening to the gunshots night and day. We escaped just as the barricades went up. Like one of those cop shows, I weaved in and around the blockades. And we have the snowball size bullet holes in the back of our car to prove

13

how close we came to not leaving. Lately, Dead Control has managed the hordes that crop up now and then. Hm, DC has a new meaning now, doesn't it? Not to be confused with the old center of government. But around here, we haven't seen a horde in two weeks and DC has done a darn good job no matter what the conspiracy theorists say."

Robert covered the kitchen floor in newspaper and placed everything else on top.

"Halloween seems to have changed its meaning, too. How I miss the benign rituals of Halloween. Getting dressed up, trick or treating, parties, haunted houses that tried to scare the bejeesus out of us. We don't need that anymore, right? One ritual is still popular, though. It goes back hundreds of years and the first part still makes my stomach churn: opening the top and scooping the slimy inside out. It has to be cleaned out well or it starts to smell quickly."

The pile grew on the newspaper. The family dog found it interesting. "Get lost, Jasper. It will make you sick."

Robert continued recording. "After ten months we returned home. Home is odd somehow…out of place. Change takes getting used to. The kids' school holds classes as usual. I don't know about where you are. If

DC spots a pack of wandering dead, the school goes into lockdown until they pass. Or, if there's enough time, they're dismissed and we are excused from our jobs without penalty to go get them. Home is safer. Stores are open for business. They just roll down their gates and wait it out. We made adjustments. And finally, we feel safe letting our guard down just for a bit to have some fun and celebrate. Like we used to."

Robert took a Sharpie and drew a design. "As you've guessed, I'm talking while I'm carving, so bear with me, listeners. This one's tougher than I expected. I gotta work with what I have and this one limits my options for creativity. Right now, I'm carving the eyes. I love doing the eyes; they're the most expressive. Round and hollow…Now the nose, and the triangle is easy enough."

He wiped off the knife and decided what to do with the mouth. The teeth are a cinch but tedious, and he cut and carved as he recorded.

"In ancient times, I was told this ritual would keep away the evil spirits. Now it just keeps away evil. What else has changed? Oh, if someone dies at home, the procedure is to call DC hotline or fill out the Request for Pickup form online. They take care of the disposal and a remembrance service is held at the house. But our neighbor's wife died and her husband, who shall remain

15

nameless for security reasons, didn't call. We found out because we heard the growling and snarling from his basement window. I told him I wouldn't call as long as he kept the chains in good order. This neighbor had a pit-bull when the kids were little. Before. I told him the same thing about the pit-bull. You can email me and tell me and other listeners what your procedures are. That's if your infrastructure is up."

Robert notched the top as a vent for the candle. He twisted and twisted the top so that it sat on the base like a puzzle piece.

"Trick or treating. Now that was fun. Free candy, dressing up as superheroes. It's too dangerous to let your kids go out now. Not so much because of the hordes. It's more because of the lone, missed strays. People have house parties instead. You're one of the lucky ones to be invited. Social out-casting hasn't gone away. Some things haven't changed. Our family was intact when we returned from the cabin. Many families weren't so fortunate, and now whispers that we had some kind of secret cure or unfair immunity keeps us from being included. We just left before it got to us. No magic there."

Robert rolled up the newspaper and admired his work. "I'm done. Not bad, kiddies. I'll post a picture on my site when it's sitting in front of my house. When the candle is inside, it will glow on our porch and remind others of Halloween's new meaning."

Robert clicked the recorder just as his kids entered the kitchen. His oldest, Tasha, stood before him with her hands on her hips. "Hey, nice! Particularly gruesome this year, Dad."

Robert smiled and nodded. "I have to agree."

Tasha's younger sister, Hannah, struggled with a large orange pumpkin as big as her own head.

Robert reached out to take it from her but she turned away. "You're going to give yourself a hernia, Hannah."

Hannah set it down on the floor and said, "How 'bout going old school this time, Dad — use a pumpkin."

Here There Be Dinosaurs

Average Read Time: 1 min 45 sec.

Sam Middleschmidt believed in dinosaurs. Not just that they lived 65 million years ago, but that they were here today still and dwelled in the 627 acres of Blydenberg Park among the weekend warrior campers and Cub Scout outings. Sam endured years of teasing trying to convince everyone they existed. But today was their 6th grade science trip to study the flora and fauna of Long Island and everyone was about to find out that Sam Middleschmidt was right.

****

The bus ride to the park was an hour away and pure torture for Sam. He was a captive punching bag for the boys who could not subscribe to the belief that dinosaurs lived on an island of New York State.

Finally, Ms. Miller the science teacher moved him to her seat at the front of the bus. "Ignore them, Sam." She patted his hand. "But you have to admit, you're asking them to accept the idea of existing dinosaurs when the only real dinosaur relatives today are birds."

"But they do exist. I saw them. Their favorite candy is red Starburst."

Ms. Miller nodded and swore when she got back, a call to the school psychologist was in order.

After an hour of walking in the woods, Sam fell behind. The boys dropped back as well and surrounded him. "Raarr, Sam." Since kindergarten they dished out hearty, daily doses of Sam Humiliation. He was used to it.

He turned in the circle. "There are *to* dinosaurs and they don't like it when you make fun of them."

"They don't eat red Starbursts, Middleshit."

"They do. It's their favorite."

"So where are they, Middleshit?"

Sam turned his head to a fog about fifty feet in front of them. "There. They're in there. You have to walk through the mist with me."

The giggles and shoving included Sam and they followed him.

"Maybe they want a Starburst," pulling at Sam's bag and laughing. "Rarrr, give me Starburst!"

Without so much as a growl from the blur, sliced and diced pre-pubescent body parts spiraled around Sam.

Ms. Miller followed the screams and passed through the veil. "Oh, my God. Sam, what happened?"

"It was a Velociraptor."

"There are no dinosaurs!"

"Oh, Ms. Miller. You shouldn't have said that."

A twig snapped behind her and she spun to see a toothy grin, one claw picking a Starburst wrapper from its teeth and another sliced her down her middle.

It's Time

Average Read Time: 1 min 40 sec.

It wasn't what we expected. The zombie outbreak was different than what we were told it would be. The Turn changed people but not into the mindless, flesh-easting creatures of pop culture lore. These zombies were thinking. They were planning. And unless you saw their eyes, really saw them, you couldn't tell they were infected.

It started Monday morning when Katie and I were walking to first period English. We were behind Mr. Woodrow, the science teacher. He was carrying a box under his arm and we noticed something dripping from the corner. It left a red liquid trail at our feet. I stopped and rubbed it with my flip flop. It was blood. Bits of hair mixed in. Horrified, we caught up and stopped him.

"Mr. Woodrow, this is going to sound psychotic but I think there's blood dripping from your box."

His strange hollow eyes looked through me.

Those eyes.

And he said, "None of your concern, Emily. Continue to class." An equally hollow grin revealed blackened teeth. "Your teacher is waiting."

A chill tingled my spine (really – like the cliché) and I retreated. Then he added, "There is no reason to resist."

It had begun.

My survival kit in my locker needed to be amended. Now, it needed to be hidden. Katie and I ran to her locker, then to mine and emptied the supplies into our backpacks:

Matches, lighter, pocket knife, bandages, antibiotics, water, beef jerky and two packages of Lunchables.

We cruised past the cafeteria on our way to English and grabbed plastic forks and knives, avoiding the cafeteria ladies' eyes. As a last minute thought, we pulled the wires from the TV's. We could use them to tie door knobs or bind teachers to their chairs.

Or wind it around their necks.

The custodian left a broom leaning against the wall. And without a word, we broke the handle into two three foot lengths. Some students walked past us with puzzled looks. Others nodded knowingly and patted their backpacks.

We continued to English class. I placed my hand on the doorknob and looked at Katie. Then I noticed the students who stood before their classroom doors. They nodded to me and I to them. They were ready, too. We took a deep breath and entered the class.

It's begun.

Shunned and Stunned

Average Read Time: 1 min. 20 sec.

Taka scratched the hair on his face and found a creepy crawly thing made its home there. How long had he been out? He pinched the thing with many legs, flicked it aside, and stood up to let the ferns, leaves and branches drop to the ground. The trees whizzed around him. He thought he was going to be sick.

"Hm. Mushrooms. Not good for Taka. Scaring off herd. Not good for Taka either."

He stumbled against a tree and grabbed hold for support. "Taka not see smelly animal with white stripe until it smell. Yelling not good for hunt."

He listened for his clan. A silent forest reminded him that they were gone. He picked up a trail of hoof prints, broken branches and nibbled leaves. Deer.

"I find food — they welcome Taka. Taka will be great leader." He notched his walking stick to count the days of his hunt, just in case.

After four notches, Taka lost the trail of the deer and lost his sense of direction to find his clan. He was alone. Or was he? Smoke billowed between the trees up ahead. Could it be? Could it be his people?

"Maybe they miss Taka. Welcome Taka anyway."

He made his way to a clearing with a small fire and cave. Cave? "That not a cave."

He tilted his head as he did not recognize this kind of small cave; it was not attached to rock. "Taka's shelter is cave in rock."

Just as he stepped out from the bushes, something came out of the cave that was not a cave.

"Dad, bring the sticks for marshmallows."

The Something froze. "Oh. My. God. Dad…Bigfoot wears deerskin!"

Perfect Dates are Over-rated

Average Read Time: 3 min.

Quiet Cove Lake
11:36 pm

*P*eter sat at the edge of the lake, lotus style and serene. He ignored the dampness seeping through the butt of his pants because this was a perfect spot. Really, truly ideal. He knew he couldn't be seen as he disappeared into the inky landscape.

He was one with nature. The frogs proved it. They talked to him, called his name. "Peter. Peter. Peter." Then they'd say, "Rachel. Rachel. Rachel."

Doesn't she hear them calling? No, of course not. She's across the lake bathed in the warm light of the cabin with that loser holding her, making wet kissy noises in her ear.

He removed a zip bag from his pocket.

26

Snip. Snip. Snip.

Other than the frogs, his nail clipper was the only sound that echoed across the still water. He thought she was perfect.

Why wasn't that enough?

He told her numerous times that her profile on Date to Mate was perfect. So was his. She said he looked like that Dolce & Gabbana model. "That's because it's me."

Lie.

They were a perfect match. Not like the others.

Snip. Snip. Snip.

And they had two perfect dates. Afterwards he sent flowers, a heart-felt email, and a necklace he made of macramé. She didn't return his calls.

Yesterday she agreed to meet him at the Panera Bread in Union Square.

She was hesitant at first but I said, "Please." Nicely.

Rachel knew the tall, blonde server Josh, and Peter noted that Panera Boy spent way too much time staring at Rachel.

My Rachel, dude.

He ordered the same thing as Rachel, Chicken and Quinoa Salad.

And what the hell is quinoa, anyway?

After tolerating Peter staring at her across the table, Rachel put down her fork and broke the perfect silence. "Okay, what did you want to talk about, Peter?"

He got down on one knee next to their Whatever Salad and she said, "You're kidding, right?"

"Uh, not really."

"We had two dates."

"This is three. Third time's a charm, isn't it?"

"Wow."

He was so excited by her reaction. "I know!"

"No. I mean like 'Wow, you're nuts.' You don't marry someone after two dates."

"Three."

She excused herself to go to the ladies room and after an excruciatingly long four minutes, Panera Boy delivered a scribbled note on a napkin. "Dude, she

28

slipped out the service entrance," and he cleared her space. Peter chewed his thumbnail. Then he took out his zip bag and snipped, much to the displeasure of the other patrons.

She mentioned she was going out of town this weekend.

A PeopleFinder search turned up a secondary address for her in Sherman, Connecticut. His rental car was a piece of crap Fiat and hoped he wouldn't end up on some countrified road, stranded with just his audio books and Fruit Roll-ups to keep him company.

His GPS was accurate and he arrived after sunset. Now he sat at the very edge of the lake where his lotus position was cutting off the circulation to his feet. He had a perfect view inside Rachel's cabin. Truly perfect. He was a genius to find her. He watched as she threw her head back in laughter.

She laughed like that with me last week. Panera Boy is so funny, isn't he?

Snip.

Peter pulled himself back from his last-week-perfect-date memory. He had to focus. See, he was patient. Oh, so patient. He could wait all night.

But he didn't have to wait much longer. His sense of time was impeccable and he knew it was getting late. He collected the clippings from his lap and sprinkled them in the zip bag. Nice addition to his collection. Then the cabin light winked out. He looked up and smiled. *See? Perfect.* The night *was* on his side and as Peter walked among the frogs, he whistled a merry tune to the beat of their croaking, indifferent to the fact that it would be a dead give-away of his presence.

****

The anonymous call the next morning tipped the police off to a double murder in the sleepy town of Sherman, Connecticut. They arrived to a grisly sight: a tall, blonde young man propped up in a kitchen chair and a fabulously attractive brunette next to him with two orders of Chicken and Quinoa salads set in front of them. And they noticed her shiny red nails were freshly…snipped.

The Four O'Clock Cheese Platter

Average Read Time: 3 min 15 sec.

Finally her two fat aunts were quiet. Now, maybe she could get a word in edge-wise. They sat there in their floral moomoos, sticking to the plastic covered furniture in the Brooklyn August heat. Mary Ellen cut a piece of cheese and placed it on a stale Triscuit and offered it to one of them. No? Sure, now they don't say anything. But it was all different about two and a half minutes ago.

"What are we going to do with you, Mary Ellen?" said Aunt Number One in her ancient purple dress.

"Yes, what are we going to do?" said Aunt Number Two in yellow.

Mary Ellen pulled at the rip in the plastic on the wing-back chair and remained silent.

31

"We set her up with a nice young man," said Aunt Lucy smoothing her purple Hawaiian print, "and what does she do?"

"Yes, what does she do?" said Aunt Rose.

"She ruins everything, Rose. Everything. All the time."

"Yes. ALL the time."

"Well, what do you expect? There's nothing in that head of hers." Lucy swivels her torso to Mary Ellen. "Shake your head, dear. See? Nothing but eyeballs."

"He exposed himself in the movie theater," said Mary Ellen.

Aunt Lucy yawned. "Well, perhaps he forgot to zipper, dear."

"Oh, yes. Boys are always forgetting that."

"Oh, yes," said Aunt Lucy with a finger digging into her ear.

Mary Ellen recognized the ridiculousness of that statement, as are most of their statements. "He's thirty-six years old."

"And you're thirty-two," pouted Aunt Lucy and she waggled her finger at Rose. "She should know better."

"Oh, yes. She should know better."

"He delivers your groceries," Mary Ellen mumbled.

"Well, that is much better than that David boy you were seeing," said Aunt Lucy.

"Oh, yes. We couldn't have that," said Aunt Rose. "He was...Mexican, after all." Aunt Rose heaved her monumental frame to the edge of the seat and cut a slice of cheese and placed it on a cracker. Mary Ellen watched as the crumbs dusted her yellow flowers. Her aunt didn't notice. Or didn't care.

"Oh, no. That would never have been acceptable," said Aunt Lucy. "Her parents would have been appalled at that relationship."

Mary Ellen tried again. "He was from Puerto Rico and he was a translator for the United Nations."

"Surely, not American then. Puerto Rico. My goodness, Rose."

"Yes, my goodness, Lucy. Could you have imagined what her parents would have thought?"

33

"We take her in after her parents were killed in that awful car accident."

Rose shifted, the plastic sticking to her meaty thighs. "Yes, just awful. Our poor sister. And this is the thanks we get."

"For twenty years, we sacrificed and worried over her well-being. Even putting her in that *place* for a year when she tried to kill herself."

"Oh, just awful. Maybe we shouldn't have mentioned it to that Mexican boy, dear."

Lucy feigned embarrassment and covered her mouth, "Oh, dear. Maybe not."

"It was a hospital." Mary Ellen felt the heat of the day stifling her, almost as oppressive as her aunts. Their chatter became a drone of muffled complaints. And her head began to hurt. She rubbed her eyes.

Shut up! Shut up!

Mary Ellen leaned over the four o'clock cheese platter.

Lucy giggled, "Oh, look, Rose. She's going to take a slice of cheese."

"It's about time she ate. She's so skinny. That's probably why that Mexican boy left anyway."

"Oh, yes. Who wants a skeleton to hold at night?"

"Oh, scandalous, dear. You're simply scandalous!"

And they laughed. And the plastic crinkled. And their fat bellies jiggled like Santa Claus' bowl full of jelly.

Mary Ellen found the knife in her hand. She turned it and admired the floral design on the silver handle. This was from her mother's set. The edge caught a glint of the summer sunlight.

Then she leaned over and sliced Aunt Number One's throat. The other one, in shock, simply had a look of horror as Mary Ellen sliced her open like a…

"A butchered cow," she thought.

Now they were quiet. Finally.

Mary Ellen placed the knife back on the tray. Mustn't stain the table. It didn't have plastic on it. Good thing the furniture did; it would make cleaning up so much easier.

Tidbits

The Orchard

Average Read Time: 6 min.

"Don't sit under the apple tree
with anyone else but me,
no, no, no…"

The Andrews Sisters echoed through the trees in the orchard and penetrated the windows of the Gallagher house. Mary and Doug Gallagher were dismayed once again that their Connecticut windows shook with the daily echo of the apple tree wartime song.

"Cripes, Mary," said Doug. "We thought, what could be more serene than living next to an apple farm. I hear that freakin' song in my sleep."

"I called the local precinct again and they tell me they go out there and complain to Mr. Donegan. But, you know, his family's been here since the Pilgrims. They won't really do anything."

37

"Pass the milk, please."

Mary handed him the small pitcher without even looking up from her tablet. "Did you see a girl in the area disappeared?" After she waited what she thought was an appropriate amount of time, "Doug, did you hear me?"

"Yeah, I heard. Another disappearance. Our town and the next seem to be some kind of black hole for missing people. And so much for bucolic living. We should have taken our chances in Queens. I could get used to buses and subways and honking horns. Cripes, this music is enough to drive me insane. And it's always the same song." Doug shamelessly referred to himself as the Highly Evolved Displaced New Yorker and, although they agreed to move to the country, he considered Queens actual royalty and all the residents of Winstead, Connecticut the common serfs. Mary, ever tolerant of her husband's delusions of grandeur, knew he meant it when he said they should have stayed in the city.

Mary finished off her coffee with a slurp. "He hung bull horns all over the orchard. I guess he likes the song when he works."

"It's crazy."

"That must be why they call him Crazy Old Man Donegan."

Doug looked at her as if that was the most asinine statement he'd ever heard.

"Don't go walkin' down Lover's Lane
with anyone else but me,"

Doug covered his ears. "Oh, my God. Make it stop!"

"no, no, no…"

Mary got up from the table and cleared her plate and her husband's.

"Hey, I'm not done."

"Yes, you are. Before you head off to work, stop by Mr. Donegan's and ask him to keep the music lower at least."

"If the police can't do anything, why would you think I can?"

"Because you're the neighbor. He should respect his neighbors."

The music stopped and so did the window rattling . Doug rubbed his eyes and sighed. "Fine. I'll walk over and come back for my stuff." And Doug Gallagher, the Highly Evolved Displaced New Yorker, walked out of his kitchen door into the bucolic morning fog never to be seen again.

****

The community came out in large groups to search the four acres of the Gallagher property and the adjacent Donegan orchard. The police organized everyone into search parties with specific areas to cover.

Crazy Old Man Donegan at first refused to let anyone on his property. "Can't have all these people traipsing through here like they own the place." But he had nothing to hide.

The Winstead police officer was losing patience with the old man. "Mr. Donegan, your neighbor was on his way to speak to you about the music. Did you see him earlier this morning?"

Donegan poked his shovel into the ground. "I told ya. I ain't seen no one this morning. I was in the orchard checkin' them trees, lookin' for the ready ones."

"And Mr. Gallagher was never here."

"You got mud in your ears, son? I said, no one was here this morning."

Officer Palamino closed his notepad and wandered past the old man to the edge of the orchard. "You know, Mr. Donegan, you always have the best looking apples. What's your secret?"

"Old family farming tricks. Generations of skill and love, son. I open the stand next week."

"Well, the town can hardly wait. The apple cider is to die for."

"Well, that's a fine New England compliment. A *fine* New England compliment."

The officer called over his radio to bring in all the search teams. They were moving on. Mary heard that and approached Officer Palamino.

"You can't call off the search. Maybe he fell in a hole and is unconscious or something. Maybe he's lost in the acres and he doesn't hear us. It's going to get cold tonight. He's here. My husband is here somewhere. He walked to the orchard and now he's gone."

"He could be one more person who's just gone missing, Mrs. Gallagher. We'll keep looking but we have ourselves a number of people who've gone missing. Just like that. Never to be seen again. Like the Bermuda Triangle only…north. We have that girl from Wicker Falls who's gone missing, too."

Mary moved in close to Office Palamino's face. "He. Is. Here. I know it."

The officer was uncomfortable under her gaze. "Go home and wait, Mrs. Gallagher. We're on this."

The volunteers gathered at the entrance to the orchard. Officer Palamino checked with the team leaders that everyone was present and accounted for. Calls of "check" followed one after the other.

Mary read the sign for the millionth time since they moved in:

"Donegan Farm. Apples from Heaven. Family owned since 1854."

She sighed in frustration. *They're not going to do shit.*

****

After she returned to the house, she decided she would go back to the orchard on her own. She had an hour or so of daylight left but she took a flashlight anyway.

"I can't wait for these people. No sense of urgency. People just disappearing all over the place. This is crazy. Like a Twilight Zone episode. Where's the FBI?"

Mary wasn't talking to anyone except the ghosts of ancient Winstead. She slammed drawers and cabinets looking for a notepad and pen. Finally she found a holiday sticky pad and scribbled:

"I'm going to the orchard to look for Doug.
He's there. And if I'm not back, I am too.
Mary."

She snapped on the porch light so she could find her way home through the orchard and then locked the front door. Whether the light was on or not, it wouldn't have mattered. Because Mary didn't come home either.

When Mary didn't show up for work the next day, police were dispatched to the house where they found her note stuck to the fridge. The police mobilized with extra patrol cars coming in from neighboring Wicker Falls. They descended upon Donegan's Orchard with a search warrant, shovels and picks. Crazy Old Man

43

Donegan played the music and rocked in his chair, "You ain't gonna find nothin' 'cause there ain't nothin' to find."

Officer Palamino stood in front of Mr. Donegan. "I don't like this anymore than you do. I came here and picked apples on my field trips for school. But something is funny going on here, Mr. Donegan, and I don't know if you're involved or not."

Donegan chuckled and rocked and sang along. "Don't sit under the apple tree, whoa, with anyone else but me. No honey. He- he."

The song ended and looped again. Finally, the officers revolted and demanded the song be shut off. And the digging continued into the early evening. The moon rose up over the eastern part of the orchard and the light shone on the red apples, making little sparkles that twinkled like newborn stars.

"Look at them beauties!" called Donegan. "Bet you ain't never seen perfection like that."

The officers looked at the old man like he was crazy which, of course, they were beginning to think the rumors were true.

"Wait for it, friends," shouted Donegan. "They're coming. The moonlight is magic. It sends its life force and blesses my orchard."

The moon-kissed apples on the trees trembled. Not the trees; the apples themselves. The officers stopped digging, dropped their tools and stepped back.

"Holy shit," said Officer Palamino. He rubbed his eyes. "What the hell *is* that?"

They watched as the apples undulated and swelled beneath the shiny red skin. They transformed into horrifying, recognizable shapes. Faces. Many faces stretched with McIntosh skin. Morphed noses and black hollow sockets for eyes. Waves of hair crested and ebbed. Mouths distorted into silent screams.

"Mother of God." Officer Jane Amelio grew pale. "It's the girl from Wicker Falls." Officer Amelio darted to another tree and got sick.

"Holy crap, Palamino. Is that a German Shepherd?" asked one of the other officers. He joined Officer Amelio and puked up his Italian Subway sandwich which landed on top of her broccoli and cheese soup mound.

Disbelief, profanity, and blue uniforms streaked past Officer Palamino and headed for the parking lot.

Donegan laughed. "He-he. Only the ones touched by the light show their faces. Mm-hm. Touched by the light."

He was right. Most looked like ready-to-eat fruit but some mutated into nightmarish howls of pain and torture.

"That's Doug Gallagher," said Officer Palamino. "That one is his wife."

Crazy Old Man Donegan beamed with pride. "Old farming tricks, son. Generations of skill and love." And he whistled his favorite tune as he rocked.

The Wish Giver

Average Read Time: 8 min.

Norbert LoneEagle smiled behind the dusty curtain and turned to the shadow behind him. "It's so easy. They're all so predictable, aren't they? Even though they're what…21, 22? All you have to do is say 'party' and they come like dogs to treats."

One by one, five socially disconnected former Busby High School attendees passed through the threshold of the house. Norbert greeted them and thanked them all for coming to his very special twenty-first birthday.

"Hey. Geronimo. What. Is. Up?" Brian Bristol, former star soccer player, punctuated each word with a finger poke to Norbert's back. Norbert was ready for it and braced himself.

Racy Tracy Rummor entered and the back of her neck was tingling. She wasn't sure why. These weren't her friends, except Mathilda who followed her in, and Mathilda insisted she come. Norbert LoneEagle never had many (any) friends. But Norbert didn't make any effort to make friends either, isolating himself and pontificating on the subject of "his family's stolen native land." Not the way to really endear himself to peers or society in general.

The final two guests, twins Daniel and Jeremiah Warfield, slapped their feet into his pant butt as they passed him. "Hey, Lone Star. Thanks for the invite, dude. Can't think of anything else I would rather do on a Friday night." They pushed each other and high-fived Brian. The unusual circumstance seemed to have bonded them.

Norbert closed the door behind them and locked it. He gestured for them all to sit and expressed his delight that they were all willing to attend. Then he disappeared into the kitchen.

The odd mix of Busby Regional High School graduates sat among the floating dust particles, waiting. They really had nothing in common except they all knew Norbert LoneEagle from school. They were never in the same classes, they hadn't played sports together and - heaven forbid - certainly wouldn't have associated with one another. But they each received the gilded invitation to Norbert LoneEagle's gathering at his house.

The envelopes were all hand delivered, with gorgeous flowing calligraphy spelling out their names.

"Your presence is hereby requested to attend the Momentous Birthday for Norbert LoneEagle. Only your attendance is expected. Please, no gifts."

As cars pulled up, he heard their comments of surprise, embarrassment and gests of curiosity to attend a Norbert LoneEagle Loser Party.

Now, in the uneasy silence of this sparsely decorated living room, they each wondered if curiosity was unlucky for more than the feline variety.

Norbert returned with a chocolate cake and burning candles. "Here we go."

Racy Tracy had been looking around and she didn't like the smell of the house. The mustiness attached to her clothes in the few minutes she was there. And the house reeked of wet dog and urine. She rubbed her nose. "Where's your dog?"

Norbert spun the plate so everyone could read the Happy Birthday words. "I don't have a dog."

Tracy leaned over to Mathilda and whispered in her ear. Mathilda rolled her eyes. Tracy returned the roll. Mathilda had these frog-eyes so large that one would be afraid to hug her for fear they'd pop right out. They were her most expressive mode of communication. Racy Tracy had other forms of communication.

"Sing," announced Norbert. But it was more of an order than a polite request.

"Where's your family? Are your parents here?" asked Tracy.

"They're around here somewhere."

But they weren't.

Norbert started to sing and waved his hand like a conductor. The girls giggled and joined in, Brian was next and the twins barked out the traditional song.

Norbert LoneEagle closed his eyes, made a wish and blew out the candles.

"What did you wish for, Tonto?" asked Brian the Great.

Norbert didn't answer.

The twins bounced their feet as a subtle threat. Norbert stared, mesmerized. Their feet were their weapon of choice when they used to corner him on the school playground. But he was safe here. In this house. His friend was with him.

"Is this how American Indians celebrate their birthdays?" Tracy wanted to know because this whole situation was making her feel very uncomfortable.

The twins burst into laughter, "Freak party for a loser."

Brian laughed with them and said, "Why did you invite us, Key-Mo-Sa-Be? No presents. No decorations. No music."

"How 'bout a rockin' DJ? We can invite the rest of our old high school buds," said Jeremiah.

"No," said his brother. "How 'bout a pow-wow?"

"I do have entertainment planned. But not quite yet."

Norbert reached under the table and pulled out an unnecessarily large meat cleaver. "Who wants a flower?"

"Oh, me," said Tracy.

Brian took out his phone to check for texts and the time.

"Uh, no phones, please," said Norbert as he dished out chocolate slices. "I'd like your undivided attention. Trade ya'. I hand you cake, you hand me your phones."

Again, it was not a request. And he had a very large knife.

They looked at each other as they surrendered their link to the outside world.

Tracy looked at her piece of cake and wondered if Norbert put something in it. She didn't eat until he did. She took one bite, put her fork down and whispered into Mathilda's ear. She rolled her eyes. Mathilda put her fork down and gulped down one of the cloyingly sweet flowers. Brian and the twins saw the girls were not eating and they stopped, too.

"I see you're all done," said Norbert. He started to collect the full plates. "What a waste of food. Not that any of you would care," and he disappeared into the kitchen.

Silent conversations passed among the guests. The oddness was truly evolving into weirdness. Mathilda rolled her eyes, and Tracy had that tingle on the back of her neck again.

Norbert returned to the living room, and lip-reading and hand gestures froze. "Ah, what's a party without entertainment, right?"

"Alright," shouted Daniel Warfield. "Tracy, get up on that table and dance. Woo!"

"Shut up, you idiot."

"No. We'll have none of that," reassured Norbert. "The entertainment has to do with the wish I made when I blew out my candles. Don't we all make wishes?"

"What was your wish, Geronimo?" said Brian.

"That the Wish Giver would come."

"The Wish Giver," said Mathilda. This was the first time she spoke. "What the hell is the Wish Giver?"

"So glad you asked, Mathilda. My ancestors from the Lakota tribe lived on this land which is now our town Busby, Montana. When they were overrun by traders and settlers, they called upon the spirit of the Wish Giver. The Wish Giver came and wiped out their settlements. And the tales of spirit protecting these lands kept others away for many years after that. The Wish Giver spirit has protected our people ever since."

The twins snorted.

"We're not here for a history lesson, Tonto," said Jeremiah.

"No, you're right. Shall we get started?"

"What is that behind you?" and Tracy pointed to a dark, amorphous shadow slink up behind Norbert.

"This…is the Wish Giver."

All of them climbed up on the furniture.

"What's going on, Norbert?" demanded Brian.

"Oh, so nice that you've addressed me by my given name, Brian. Thank you." He moved about the room and around his guests. "I didn't ask you all to bring gifts, I know." He paused. "But it doesn't mean you aren't going to give me presents."

The shadow floated around the room and the front door dissolved into a solid wall. The shadow passed the windows, the staircase and the entrance into the kitchen, and they watched their emergency exits all disappear. Panic set in and Norbert's guests pounded on the walls.

"You all have so much to give," said Norbert ignoring his guests' annoying displays of distress. "Let's start with you, Brian. You have no idea how infuriating your finger poke was every time you passed me in the halls. Ten years of finger pokes. Finger pokes and calling me any Indian name your cramped, intolerant mind could find."

Brian crouched behind the girls' backs. "I'm sorry, Norbert. It was just a joke. Really."

"Mmm, too late," and Norbert waved his hand. "You first."

The Wish Giver engulfed Brian's whole body in a mass of blackness. He let out a scream. When the shadow floated back to Norbert, it placed a finger on the coffee table.

Brian stood up to find his poking pointer finger missing. No blood. Just missing. The girls screamed and the twins ran around the room still looking for an exit. Even the fireplace was gone.

"Beautiful, Brian. Thank you for your present. Let's see. Who's next?"

They all stopped dead still. "Uh, Tracy. You're always whispering. Whispering, whispering. Never having the courage to say your insults out loud. Now you don't have to say them at all."

The Wish Giver shot over to Tracy before she could move and swallowed her as it did Brian. Tracy let out a screech and began to sob. Her hands covered her mouth and, again, there was no blood.

The Wish Giver returned to Norbert and placed Tracy's tongue on the table. "Perfect, Tracy. Thank you."

He faced Mathilda. "You. You say nothing but your eyes speak volumes. Guess what you'll be giving me for my birthday?"

55

Mathilda shoved Brian in front of her as if that would help. The shadow shot over to her next and covered her face. When it moved away, her eyes were gone. They sat next to the finger and the tongue.

"Oh, my God," said Daniel. "Jeremiah, do something."

"You do something. You're older by two minutes."

Norbert smiled. He was so happy it was his birthday. "Since you are twins, a twin gift would only be appropriate."

The Wish Giver covered their legs and they fell on their backs. "No!"

The shadow returned to the table and Norbert seemed surprised. "Oh, I have a pair. One left and one right foot. Thank you, Wish Giver. That was quite considerate."

The spirit floated one final time around the room and hovered over the cowering guests. Then it melted into the walls, Norbert LoneEagle's wishes granted.

Norbert adored the gifts on his table, "Thank you all for your presents. I couldn't have asked for a better birthday. I think they were all well-deserved, don't you? You can all go now."

He threw their phones on the couch, and the doors and windows appeared. Brian, Tracy and Mathilda ran to the door. The twins hopped. Brian being the first there, slid the latch and pushed the others aside.

An hour and a half later, police and news vans arrived at an abandoned house. In fact, it looked as if no one had lived in the mid-century cape for years. That's because no one had. The town knew this house had been empty for at least three years after the LoneEagle family left. The police searched the bedrooms but they were empty of clothes, and all the rooms were bare of personal belongings. They used black light looking for blood. How could any of this happen without buckets of blood all over the place? Nothing. They questioned the kids numerous times at the hospital; their stories did not waiver. Regardless, the police intimated that drugs were involved. Empty houses are an attraction for nefarious behaviors. And no shock for this crew.

There was just no sign of Norbert LoneEagle. Captain Blackfoot assured the news people and advised the other officers that he would personally investigate Norbert LoneEagle's mysterious disappearance, if he had indeed returned, or whoever else was involved.

But he wouldn't.

Amid the circus of press vans, lights and officers' repeated statements of "No comment," Captain Blackfoot excused himself and made one more sweep of the interior. Alone and in the quiet of the house, he knew. He entered the kitchen and noted smudges on the white Formica. He ran his fingers on the counter, rubbed them together and took a whiff. Sweet. He wiped away the remnants of chocolate icing and licked his fingers.

Chocolate icing was his favorite.

Long Live Wilbur March

Average Read Time: 5 min.

When most people receive a diagnosis of cancer, they're devastated. Wilbur March, however, was thrilled. The fact that it was terminal was even better. It was like he hit the lottery. Now he qualified for admission into the Preservation of Life Program and he can start his life all over again.

Wilbur March was Director of Family Leave at his company. Which meant he counted the days people were out, why they were out and if their leave was actually legitimate. Everyone hated him. That was okay because he didn't like them either. His bean counting job was stressful and deliriously boring at the same time. He described his marriage the same way. When Cora wasn't a bitch, which was most of the time, she was a bore. And her mother who lived in the downstairs bedroom trained her well and made sure Cora was a carbon copy of her. And they both had this thing about the garbage sitting out.

Christ.

On Monday, the doctor said, "I'm sorry, Mr. March, there's no cure at this time. But you do qualify to have your body suspended until one is discovered. Shall I fill out the paperwork?"

"You bet."

On Tuesday, Wilbur March slapped down the flat fee of $5,256.42 in cash – including taxes – onto the receptionist's desk at the Preservation of Life offices.

The girl looked left and right, and bit the tip of pen. "No one uses paper money anymore, you know that. I'll have to run the serial numbers for all of them."

"No problem. I'll wait."

She looked nervous. "You can actually meet with one of our counselors while I do...this." And she lifted the bills as if they were contaminated.

Wilbur was directed to enter the second door on the left and see Mrs. Trimarco. He scanned the room until he saw the name plate on the desk.

"Mrs. Trimaco? I'm Wilbur March and I'm dying."

"Oh. Oh, well, please have a seat, Mr. March. Let's see what we can do. Are you familiar with Body Suspension?"

"Similar to cryonics. Like Walt Disney's head is frozen somewhere. I'll be frozen until there's a cure for whatever I have."

"Actually, we've moved to a less tissue damaging procedure. A Vacuum Sealant."

"Vacuum sealed. Like smoked salmon."

"Well, uh, not exactly," and she leaned in close and whispered, "But yes."

"That's just fine. When can I be…sealed up?"

"Is your paperwork for your family in order? Because they won't be here when you awaken most likely depending if you want effective treatment or cure."

"Fuck treatment. Wake me when there's a cure."

"Okay," and Mrs. Trimarco dragged that out like when her five year old niece blurts out profanity. She waved her hand over a button and a projection keyboard appeared on her empty desk. She tapped the lighted letters and watched her screen. "Which disease do you have?"

61

"Lung cancer."

"Effective treatment and maintenance is planned to be available in about thirty years. And you could still return to familiar surroundings. For a cure," tap-tap-tap, "about 150 years."

Wilbur March was just about to burst with joy. Everyone will be gone. Cora. Her mother. His bean counting job. He could start over in a new place with new friends and a job he'd love.

Mrs. Trimarco had never seen anyone quite so giddy. "Your paperwork, Mr. March. Is it done and your next of kin notified and provided for if necessary?"

"Yes, yes, yes. When can you seal me up?"

"Well," and she tapped away on the lighted letters. "Seems we can take you as early as tomorrow."

Wilbur literally bounced in his seat. "Thank you, Mrs. Trimarco." He reached across the desk and grabbed her hand pumping it up and down, up and down. He headed for the door and said, "See you all tomorrow!"

On Wednesday, Wilbur March was vacuum sealed like a slab of smoked salmon.

****

62

Wilbur opened his eyes, turned his head and saw the numerical display on the wall: 12:35pm – April 15, 2200. *How long has it been?* His head was too foggy to run the numbers.

"Welcome back, Mr. March. I'm Dr. Amelia Sawyer, your Reintegration Therapist. You've been asleep for 145 years and you are now cancer free."

"Where am I?"

"You are at the Preservation of Life storage arena. Let's get you out and off to your new life."

Oh, yeah. That's right! He smiled knowing that his former life, his crappy job and bitchy wife dissolved away naturally with time.

The attendants washed and dressed him while Dr. Sawyer brought him up to date on two wars, a toxic atmosphere and a completely hermetically sealed living environment since 2145.

"That's just fine. I hated nature anyway."

She walked him to the Waiting Station where another attendant explained how he was to get around the city. "These are pneumatic cars, Matic-Cars. You just punch in your destination and – whoosh - the pneumatic tubes take you anywhere in the city. Ready to go?"

"I don't have anywhere to go yet." He turned to Dr. Sawyer for guidance.

She dictated final notes onto her tablet then joined Wilbur next to his waiting car. "Right, Mr. March. Here you go. Your new work assignment. Librarian."

He giggled. That was just perfect. A place where he didn't have to talk to anyone.

"And your new address. Government aid will cover you until your first paycheck."

Wilbur was about to climb into the Matic-Car when Dr. Sawyer said, "And there's one more thing. I checked your next of kin list. Routine, you see, and I found your wife Cora was here as well."

What?

"Unfortunately, her disease progressed rapidly back then so all we could salvage was, well…" And an attendant rolled out a gurney with just Cora's head. Tubes of red fluid and electrodes spiraled in Medusa fashion. And it spoke.

"Hello, Wilbur-darling," and it was laced with a hint of familiar venom.

"Her payment plan ran out after about 125 years and government aid doesn't cover her as long as there's a next of kin able to do so. So she's yours now."

Only gurgles came out of Wilbur March's mouth.

"And more good news. Cora's mother was also preserved right next to her." And another gurney displayed his mother-in-law's Medusa head.

"Hello, Wilbur. Come give your mother-in-law a kiss."

Dr. Sawyer smiled at this time traveling family reunion. "Now that there is a living relative for the two of them, they will be bumped up on the body receiver list."

Great.

The attendants slid the platters in the back seat of the car.

"Someone will come by every two days for their maintenance." Dr. Sawyer handed him a jug of yellow liquid. "Make sure there is at least two inches in the tray at all times." She took his hand, "Good luck, Mr. March."

Whatever.

Wilbur climbed into the front, put his address into the screen and looked over his shoulder at the two women he despised most in the world.

And they started.

Cora sniffed. "Wilbur, did you take out the garbage? You know how I hate when it sits. There shouldn't be any garbage. The smell, oh, the smell."

"Wilbur, give your favorite mother a kiss. Do you hear me up there? Cora, did he take out the garbage?"

"I don't think he said. He's such an idiot. Wilbur, are you listening? Did you take out the garbage? You know how I hate when it sits. Wilbur, answer me. Did you take out the garbage?"

Wilbur March looked in the rear view mirror and said, "No, not yet."

Any Day Above Ground

Average Read Time: 5 min.

I open my eyes to absolute darkness and to a stale woody smell just inches from my nose. I don't remember being here, how I got here. I don't even recall where I was last. My amygdala is setting off internal alarms. I'm not in full-blown panic state yet, but I'm getting there.

I have a tendency to succumb to claustrophobia in a matter of seconds. I always have. *I remember that.* I turn my head left and right but that tells me squat. I move my arm to feel around. In just a few inches, my knuckles hit wood all around me. So close. I push on the sides. The sides are so close.

"Hey! Someone! Let me out!"

Calm yourself, Dave. Caaalm.

Dave. My name is Dave Walker. That's a good start.

This wood is so close - right in my face. My breath bounces right back to me. Do I have enough air in here? *Stop it. Stop it. Don't hyperventilate. Figure out where you are.* Think. Think. Think. Think.

I bite my lower lip to take my attention off the panic. Grit covers my mouth and I spit. *Well, that wasn't too bright, Dave. It dripped right back onto your face.* I move my hand up along my body to wipe off the spit and…dirt. It feels like dirt. Tastes like dirt. *Where the hell am I?*

I hear muffled voices.

"Hey! Help me!" But, then, they are gone. "No! Come back!"

I feel around and the damp wood is enclosing me on all sides. I can barely move my arms. I can't move around. I can't turn over or sit up. *Let me out, let me out.* I thrash my body around in hopes of, what, breaking free? But it doesn't do anything. What is this? "Hey! Where am I?"

I feel sick. *Oh my God. Don't get sick in here, Dave. Don't get sick.*

I take a few calming breaths and talk myself down. *Don't become hysterical, now.* I slide my right hand back up my chest and rub my eyes. My hand swipes something long hanging above my face. *Is it a worm? Bugs! Oh, my God! What is it? What is it?!* My hand brushes it again and I hear a faint tinkle. My fingers search for whatever the hanging thing is. It's not slimy; it's a string. A string hanging in a box. What the…?

Well, pull it, you moron. See what it does!

I yank on it and I hear a bell ring far away. "Heeey!"

A string in a box – with a person. I know why this is familiar. Yes. This is like those Scare-the-Shit-Out-of-You stories I read before bed. They used to bury people with a string attached to a bell just in case they weren't really dead. Someone would sit by the grave and the person in the coffin had three days to ring the bell to let them know they buried an alive person. After three days, I guess they supposed you were actually dead as dirt and – whoop – they'd yank the string out and well, there you have it.

I wrap the string around my fingers several times.

Is that where I am? Am I dead? But I'm not dead because I'm here. Here. In a box.

Oh, boy. Oh, boy. Here it comes. My hands are tingling. *Don't think about your breathing, Dave. Don't think. Ignore it. Don't take short breaths. In through your nose, out your mouth.* Someone buried me thinking I was dead. *I don't remember being in an accident. I wasn't sick, I don't think.* I feel around my body. No pain. All in one piece. Why would they think I'm dead? I'm not! I'm not!

I pull the string again and again, "I'm here! I'm alive! Let me out! Please! Please!"

I'm sorry, Dave. I can't do that.

They don't hear me out there. And the air is getting thinner. Less for me to breathe.

Ha! If I wasn't dead when they put me in, I will be soon, and I start to laugh. Laughing uses more oxygen. Don't laugh. *But I can't help it.* I keep ringing the bell. Why don't they hear it? I can.

And then I hear them again. Closer this time, clearer. Tight. It's so tight in here. I pound on the sides, "Hey, out there!"

"He's dreaming again, Doctor. He's pulling at the restraints."

I'm not restrained.

"He's not supposed to be doing that. Give him another dose of pentobarbital and fix his earphones.

70

And keep playing that Buried Alive recording. His incarceration is well deserved."

Incarceration. I remember now. Fifty years to life.

"This one's not eligible for parole, is he?"

I hear the doctor laugh. *He laughed.* "That's what I was told."

"Wow. We'll all be long gone when he wakes up, huh?"

But I'm awake! And I pound on the sides. "I'm here!"

"You bet. At least my tax dollars won't be going to his cable or food, and he won't play basketball all day like he's at some resort."

A buzzer goes off. "Bed 735C is waking, too."

"Which way is that?"

"That way. At the front of the building."

No! Don't go!

"God, I hate all this walking…"

Rows and rows. Rows and rows.

"Who thought making this warehouse so big was a good idea? All right, come with me, then. Which one is C? Top or bottom bed?"

"Top, Doctor. And this one should be back in coma-state in a few."

Coma-state.

I wait, hoping unconsciousness would kick in and this will disappear, melt away like they promised. The stale air is suffocating. Minutes pass that feel like a forever wait.

And then I hear the nurse, "Okay, he's out."

Out? I'm not out. I'm not out! I'm still here, in this box! Coma people are not supposed to think anything, feel anything. That's what I was told at sentencing.

"After the next one, Kate, you wanna grab a bite at Finnegan's?"

"One of their juicy burgers sounds…"

And they're gone again.

"Wait! No!" I yank on the bell. The more I scream, the more air I use up. Less and less air. The dark is oppressive and liquid tar fills my lungs. *I can't breathe. There's nothing left!*

Check off all the boxes that apply: I am most uncomfortable when…

Psychological profile, my ass.

"Mr. Walker, the prosecutor has given you the option to forego your prison sentence for Alternative Sedation, which you have taken. Congratulations."

Congratulations, the judge said.

"Piece of cake, Judge. You bald bastard."

Ha! Ha-Ha! Hold it together, Dave. You're starting to lose it.

Joke's on me, isn't it? They know. A permanent state of elsewhere.

Hold it together. You have a long way to go, Dave.

This is my fifty years to life. Fifty years in a box, underground, covered in six feet of dirt, ringing a bell no one will hear.

Oh, my God. No air. No air. No air.

You Can't Take It With You

Average Read Time: 5 min.

Wilmington Press

LOTTERY TICKET KILLS WILMINGTON MAN

On November 15, John D'Ambrosia, 64, was in the dining room of the McDonald's Restaurant on Ellerson Ave. When he realized he was the winner of the elusive $10 million dollar scratch off **Prize for Life**, he went into cardiac arrest, his face falling into the ketchup puddle next to his half-eaten Quarter Pounder with Cheese.

He was admitted into Wilmington Central Hospital where three days later he died of complications. According to family acquaintances, Mr. D'Ambrosia refused to officially claim the monetary prize and no one from his family has claimed it on his behalf.

The money will remain in escrow for one year according to state law. The Wilmington Press was unable to reach the family for comment.

St. Joseph's Cemetery
Wilmington, Delaware
November 20 - 6:45 pm

John D'Ambrosia's wife Blanche and twins Jamie and Jen stood aside his grave. They waited the past hour for the sparse collection of mourners and semi-sober priest to pay their respects and leave. Blanche huffed. *This is what Purgatory must be like.*

Jamie checked her phone and wondered how much longer she needed to stand in the dark, damp air. Her twin Jen blew out a hefty plume of smoke and then mashed the cigarette into the grass with her pleather boots.

"That is *so* disrespectful," said Jamie.

"Pick it up," snapped her mother.

Jen stared them down and didn't move. "What is that noise? It is so annoying."

Blanche looked around. "It's those squirrels chewing."

"God, it sounds like scratching. Scratching in a cemetery is just plain creepy. If I ever come here again, I'm bringing Pop's rifle and the squirrels are target practice."

"Shut up, Jen," said Jamie. "*You're* so annoying."

The only other family member to dally was John's brother Harry, the executor of his estate. He stared at his two nieces who behaved more like spoiled prepubescents than the adult women they were and wondered how his stupid brother managed to screw up both of them.

He buttoned up the collar of his coat. "Don't take it out on each other. I told you, your father was very clear he didn't want to leave anything to any of you."

Blanche took off her black veil. "He shut me out from his hospital room. Refused to see the girls. Refused to see anyone but you." And she sniffed.

Like she would cry over that, thought Harry. "He named me executor." He put up his hand, "And before you challenge that, there were witnesses when he changed his will. I showed you the paperwork."

Blanche huffed and pouted. "But to be buried *with* the scratch off. Who ever heard of something like that?"

"He had his reasons."

Jamie stepped between her Uncle Harry and her mother. "He didn't even leave the money to you, did he?"

"No, he didn't. He offered it to me but I turned it down. I'm comfortable. I'm okay." *Besides, if I took it I would have three bat shit crazy women hounding me with years of litigation.*

They were quiet for all of two and a half minutes.

Jamie kicked some dirt into the hole. "When are they going to…fill this in?"

"Tomorrow morning," answered Blanche. "Since it's Sunday night, they'll do it first thing tomorrow."

They were quiet for another two and half minutes.

Harry made the sign of the cross and bid a silent farewell to his big brother. "Ladies, I'd like to say it's been a pleasure, but it clearly wasn't." And he began to walk toward his car.

"Wait, Harry," said Blanche. "We're not going to see you again?"

"Not unless my brother rises from the grave like Jesus Christ."

"Girls, say good bye to your Uncle Harry."

They looked over their shoulders and said nothing.

"Exactly," was Harry's last word.

Blanche shot darts with her make-up caked eyes. *Son of a bitch.* "We're on our own girls. Let's go home."

And all the way to the car and all the ride home, Blanche listened to her daughters complain that Uncle Harry had no right to be executor and he probably convinced Daddy not to cash that ticket.

Blanche felt a migraine settling in.

They are so annoying, simmered Blanche. *But they are right.*

St. Joseph's Cemetery
10:45 pm

Blanche studied the depth of the grave and figured if she stood on the coffin she could pull herself up and out when she was done. "He's not being buried with ten million dollars. Whoever heard of such a thing? *I* deserve it."

She spun around with the flashlight to shine it on the chewing squirrels. "Shut up! God!"

She didn't give any thought that what she was about to do was particularly gruesome and more than a tad sacrilegious. She justified it with the narcissistic logic of a politician lying to his constituents. "It's mine."

She jumped in and landed with a hollow thump. She felt for the latch and pulled open the body section and top. "Not sure where Harry hid the ticket, sly bastard he is."

She rummaged around her husband's tweed jacket pockets and matching slacks. "Bingo."

She turned the flashlight on the paper to make sure it had the yellow arches. "Sorry, John. You can't take it with you."

Her flashlight winked out. "Oh, crap."

She slapped it several times against her palm. In the hellish dark of the grave, before she could utter a breath, a vice of fingers grabbed her upper arm, pulled her in and slammed the top shut.

11:35pm

With a menthol hanging from her lips Jen mumbled, "This has to be the most warped thing you've ever come up with, Jamie."

"He's not being buried with that ticket. We have to at least try. We'd be set."

They stood at the edge of the grave and Jamie shone the beam inside the cavernous hole. Jen doubted she could go through with this. There were some things even she wouldn't do. "This is really sick. I can't do this."

"Chicken," said Jamie.

"Not chicken. Just…more moral than you."

Jamie rubbed her temple. Jen wasn't more of anything than her. "Well, *I'm* not going in there. I thought you would just jump in and…"

"What? I would do what, Jamie? Open the top? Search the pockets of my dead father? Oh, my God. This is so gross. We're sick. We are truly sick."

Then they heard the scratching.

Slow and long. Scratch, scratch, scratch.

They froze and held their breath.

Jamie swiveled with the light and searched the trees for the squirrels. "What are squirrels doing up at this hour?" But she could see none.

Jen regretted not bringing the rifle. "That didn't sound like squirrels. That sounded…different." She *really* regretted not bringing the rifle.

Jamie pointed the beam at Jen's face. "That was a squirrel chewing like mom said."

"Uh-uhh. No, it wasn't."

Slow and long. Scratch, scratch, scratch. Slow and long.

Jen could see Jamie's hand starting to shake and Jen whispered, "I think we should leave — now."

"Yeah, maybe we should."

Jen placed her hands on her knees and bent over the hole. "Bye, Pop. I guess you are taking it with you after all."

The girls weaved through the headstones half expecting a hand to grab their ankles. When they were safely in the car, doors locked, Jamie said, "Won't Mom wonder where we've been?"

"Like she cares. Besides, I don't think she's home. She wasn't when we left."

"Where'd she go?"

"She said something about going out for a lottery ticket."

The Essence of the Portrait

Average Read Time: 10 minutes

The owner of the Prince Street Gallery walked back and forth in front of the paintings, her heels clicking on the parquet floor like a Nazi fräulein. Elliot Andrews hated her. She was mean and nasty but she liked his work and for that he was willing to tolerate her. Ilsa Strauss launched many careers with her keen eye and her spider web connections of wealthy patrons. Today he was hoping to get some time in her gallery. Elliot Andrews needed a benefactor. He wanted to live an existence that was more than just barely making his rent. He was Michelangelo and he had to find his de Medici. And soon. He had one month's rent payment left.

Ilsa Strauss stopped, hands on her hips. *Power stance*, thought Elliot.

"This can't be all you have."

Elliot decided before he came in that he wouldn't be intimidated by her. *You can be very brave in front of a mirror.* Elliot was very good at self-flagellation. *Will she see the sweat pits on my shirt? People like her smell fear. I must stink.* "I have more at home. This was just a...teaser."

"I don't like to be teased, Mr. Andrews. In any form," and her hips brushed past his backside as she walked around him.

There will be no bashtupping, Fräulein.

"Well, how many more do you have?"

Elliot wiped his upper lip with the back of his hand. Everything was riding on this meeting. "I have three more portraits at home."

"Hm. Five portraits do not a show make. I like these two here. There's a spirit about these people that transcends the canvas. I feel I can know them. That they have a history. This one you call Madeline. Her eyes are soulful, sad, as if she knows the secret of death and is waiting, resigned even." Her face was now six inches from the canvas. "Did you know her?"

"What?" Elliot's inner self had gone on hiatus to spare himself any scathing comments.

"Did you know Madeline?"

84

He had returned from the otherworld with a perfect answer. "Uh, no. I made her up. She's a composite of people. People I see on the street or in a restaurant or in Home Depot."

"That's fascinating in itself, Mr. Andrews. I thought they were models."

"That would be too easy. It's like cheating. Madeline and all my others are formed from my soul. Their souls. They are my ideal subject. I wouldn't be able to find one person with all the qualities and...essence that I want, that I need to say."

"What do you want to say, Mr. Andrews?"

"I just want my audience to feel."

Ilsa liked that answer. She liked it a lot. She had never heard that before. Usually artists gave her soliloquies that they thought she wanted to hear. Crap about starting an artistic movement or they insist on making a political statement. Artists who barely hold onto reality and border on psychosis like the Christian Haters, neo-feminists, hyper-individualists or adults who never rebelled as adolescents and now take it out on the canvas. Art can just be. That was something people misunderstood about her. She knew what they said on the street about her, and what they said about her even at her own gallery cocktail parties. But that was okay with her. She found that fair-weather artists were afraid to approach her, and so didn't waste her time, and only serious flakes had the courage to enter the lion's den.

"Relax, Mr. Andrews. I like your work. I'll give you March 25th, 26th and the 27th."

Elliot exhaled. "Thank you. That will be great."

"But like I said, you can't have a show with five pictures. Give me two more. Seven altogether. You'll share the gallery with another artist but different open house hours."

"I'll share. I'm okay with that. And I can give you two more portraits, no problem."

****

Elliot went back to his apartment and set up all five portraits, the two from his meeting and the three he left behind, set them side by side and he started.

"Madeline, you were marvelous today. You really spoke to her, the witch. Your beautiful soul just out shone her evilness."

He turned to the portrait entitled Henry. "I think The Fräulein has a penchant for girls the way she was looking at Madeline, right?"

He addressed the other three, Pamona, Pablo and Sarah. "Oh, you guys should have been there to see it. Maybe she swings that way. That's okay. I don't care. It wasn't like I was going to ask Eva Braun out for drinks. Eva Braun." And he chuckled at his clever historical reference.

Then Elliot paused as if he were listening. "Yeah, you're riiiggghht. She rubbed her meaty hip into me. Like I thought that was sexy or something."

He pulled out two blank canvases from behind his Ikea couch. "Ladies and gentlemen, it looks like more siblings will be added to our family. Ms. Strauss wants two more portraits before the show."

He listened.

"Oh, no worries, Pamona. I understand your abandonment issues. I'll love you all still. The heart grows to accommodate more in the family. Love is not divided, my precious, it's multiplied."

Elliot put on his coat and grabbed a scarf and gloves. "It's time I visit Gordy the Ghoul."

Gordy the Ghoul worked the overnight shift at the city morgue. He was twenty-three and a heroin addict who actually kept his shit together. He sustained his habit by selling the blood from his exsanguinated guests to Elliot and the delusional Satanist-slash-Vampire underworld. He welcomed any company since no one ever came to visit him. And who could blame them? So when Elliot pushed through the swinging doors, Gordy smiled, slid his latest arrival into the meat locker and slammed it shut. "Dude! Where have you been? I have liquid gold for you, man."

The smell hit Elliot like a city sidewalk after a night of drinking. Disinfectant. Coppery-blood. Febreze. "Hey, Gordy. Been busy."

"How much do you need tonight? The vampires cleaned me out yesterday. Some underground party. They invited me, but I won't go. I'm messed up, but not that messed up."

"That was probably a good move. Like you need another addiction to attend to."

Gordy laughed, "Yeah, right? You so get me, dude. We should so totally hang out some time."

"Sure, Gordy. Whenever. I need just four ounces."

"You're good for the money, yeah?"

"Aren't I always?" And Elliot flashed him a hundred dollar bill.

"Cool." Gordy stuck half his body into a large refrigerator and leaned all the way into the back. He moved bottles of labeled sciencey liquids, a can of Mountain dew and a bag from Subway. Elliot thought it was quite gross that Gordy's lunch was mixing it up with the embalming crew. Gordy was truly a ghoul.

He pulled out two labeled jars that had a serial number on each. Elliot watched with amazement as Gordy poured two ounces from each jar into skinny vials. Despite his shaky hands, Gordy managed to not spill a drop of blood. He was due for a hit soon.

"Two vials. Two ounces in each. I'll double bag them in case they leak."

"Great."

"You know, dude, I'm messed up. I say it all the time. And I know messed up shit when I see it." Gordy dropped his voice to a whisper as if the dead might revolt with what he was about to say. "Dude, painting with blood. *That's* messed up."

"Gord, my paintings have a soul because they are imbued with the essence of someone who has lived. See, I mix their soul with my acrylics to produce masterpieces that rival Rembrandt, Vermeer and Van Dyke. I have an affinity for the Dutch Masters with their use of stark lighting, saturated colors and obsessive attention to detail. They are eternal."

Elliot was missing that Gordy really didn't care. "These people were energy once. Energy cannot be created nor destroyed. Soul is energy. My paintings have captured their essence."

"Sure. Whatever you say, man."

Elliot closed in on Gordy's face and crossed the threshold of the eighteen inch boundary of personal space. He could feel Elliot's warm garlic breath hit his red, coke-lined nose. And Elliot leaned in even closer, "There's a mummy buried in my parent's backyard."

Gordy took a step back. "Really."

"Gord, I shit you not. My father was a painter. He used a paint color called Mummy Brown. Why did they call it Mummy Brown? So glad you asked."

"I didn't ask."

"Because they mixed ground up Egyptian mummies into the paints. Who would even think of that? But the mummy dust added a tonal quality to the pigments, an unearthly color somewhere between raw umber and burnt sienna. Beautiful. Rich. Ethereal. Well, my father didn't know. The color had been around for a hundred years. When the secret came out, he was utterly disgusted. Well, disgusted is really not the right word. Horrified? He dug a hole in the backyard and placed his tubes of Mummy Brown paint in the hole. My mother brought flowers and they said a prayer hoping the soul would be at peace."

"That *is* messed up."

"They stopped making the color when they ran out of mummies. No apologies, no outcry from the moral majority. The point is, sometimes you have to go to great lengths to make great art." Elliot shifted and the dark shadow on his face disappeared. "Okay, before I go, I need to know the details on my donations."

Gordy pulled a file off the desk. "This is my Elliot pile. I got a Vampire pile because they want to see the records. Make sure they're not getting any transmitted diseases."

He flipped to Vial A's sheet. "I remember her. She looked like my Gammy. Vial A is from an old lady, like 90 years old. Lived in the village in a rent controlled apartment. A hermit. She never came out, no one claimed her. Apparently a holocaust survivor. I could tell by the number tattoo on her arm."

"Physical details, Gordy. What'd she look like?"

"Caucasian. Skinny. Grey hair, blue eyes, wrinkly hands, lines on her face. You know, old lady." Then he seemed to drift away. "Lots of life there."

"What was the shape of her nose?"

"Her nose? One of those hook noses. And tight lipped, but that could because rigor mortis set in."

"Name?"

"Adelaide."

"Oh, I love that. How 'bout the other one?"

Gordy pulled out the second sheet in the folder and read off the details of a bodega owner who was shot during a robbery. "Sad. The guy had six kids. Name was Miguel."

Elliot felt he had plenty to work with. "Gordy, you did it again. You are an inspiration to a weary artist."

Gordy beamed. "Dude, we should totally hang out."

****

When Elliot got back to his apartment, he rummaged through his recyclable box and pulled out assorted empty yogurt cups. He squeezed out colors he decided to use and poured drops of the blood from the vials into the paints. He said a silent prayer for inspiration as he mixed. Then he attacked his canvas with renewed excitement.

"My children," he called over his shoulder, "no worries. You will have a new grandmother. And Pablo, you will now have someone to converse with in your native tongue."

Three weeks later, and the day before the opening, Elliot finished his Adelaide and Miguel portraits. He brought his children to the gallery and he was responsible for hanging them in whatever order he felt best represented his theme. Ms. Strauss was MIA, which was fine with him. Her nephew babysat the gallery in the evening and he was waiting for Elliot to finish. It was getting late.

"Elliot, are you almost done? It's 11:30."

"My children have to tell me where they'd like to be. The light in the gallery is very specific at night and my opening is tomorrow night. And I still have to hang my name and bio."

"I have to go," and he shoved in a mouthpiece with extended canines, "or else there won't be anything left for me."

"Yeah. Sure. Go."

Vampirina tossed Elliot the keys and told him to just bring them the next day. He pushed through the door and disappeared into the night like a true phantom.

Ilisa Strauss' midnight arrival was unexpected. Elliot was cleaning up the brown paper, tape and assorted measuring tools.

"Well, well. How's my protégé?" She slinked in closer to him than he was comfortable with.

No, behave, mein meister-ette.

She made her way past all the portraits and stopped at the last one entitled, Adelaide.

"Do you like her?" Elliot asked.

Ilsa didn't answer right away. "Is this some kind of statement because of my name?"

"What do you mean?" He began to panic.

"Adelaide has a concentration camp marking on her forearm."

"No, that's who she is - was. It's just part of her life story. Made her who she was up until the day she died. No statement. No statement."

Ilsa nodded, reassured at least for the moment. "I saw the gallery lights still on and that you were still here working." She paused. "I live across the street. That apartment there with the cat in the window."

Not engaging.

"Did my nephew leave the keys with you?"

"Your nephew had...an appointment."

"I know his appointments. Blood, gore, and humiliation seem to run in my family."

Elliot wasn't sure what she implied with that bit of information.

Not engaging.

"I'll be here at six tomorrow night to help set up."

"I'll be here at seven." Ilsa swept by him. He smelled her lavender perfume and felt her female energy pass through him like ghosts of Fuhrer-women past. He was happy when she left. She was a distraction. He had just his name and bio plaque left to do.

As he was about to stick a Commando hook to the wall, the lights went out. A familiar coppery smell filled the room. He reached out like a blind person, feeling for the light switch and snapped it on and off, on and off. Shuffling came from behind him and from around the pillars. He spun left and right.

"Who's there?"

His pounding heart drowned out his ability to think. But he heard the whispers.

"You made us real, Elliot."

"Yes, you gave us life. But not Life we wanted."

He knew the voices; he heard them innumerable times before. Madeline. Henry.

"Elliot, I hoped to rest. It was my time to rest." Adelaide, tired of existing.

"I wanted to be with my real family, but you kept me from them. Alone here." Pamona, her voice laced with fear of being left behind.

The other three voices surrounded him in the din of whispers, all speaking at once.

"Release us. Release us."

Elliot felt tears and sorrow well up from his core and he spoke to the dark. "My children, I immortalized you. I blessed your images with your essence."

"You stole our essence," the voice Sarah was angry that she hadn't moved on. "I've waited so long."

In unison, "We've waited so long."

"No, this is a good thing. You will live forever. Here on this canvas. For all to worship what you have given to this world with your sacrifice. Madeline, you've given us your beauty and deep appreciation for life. Henry, you...you taught me how to recognize my authentic self. Miguel and Pablo, you were brave when faced with fear."

"We have very little time."

"No, listen. Sarah and Pamona, sisters separated by time and space. You loved living even when fear gripped your lives. Adelaide. You were exemplary in showing us that life prevails even after experiencing monsters worse than the human imagination. I appreciate all of you, don't you see that?"

"No more."

"It's time you join us."

Elliot was begging now. "No. No. I'm not done."

The invisible energies surrounded him. Blackness smothered him whole and sucked the air from his lungs. And then...nothing.

Ilsa Strauss arrived at the gallery at seven the next evening, lights out, doors locked.

He should have been here setting up. Flakey artists.

Ilsa unlocked the door, pulled it open and Elliot's body lay at the foot of his portraits. His life puddled into the crevasses of the parquet floor, and hand and fingerprints marked the surrounding area. Ilsa's mouth opened but nothing came out. She fumbled for the gallery phone and dialed 911.

"He's dead! He's dead!" She listened. "I don't know what happened. There's blood all over him….His name? Uh, Elliot Andrews...153 Prince Street. The Prince Street Gallery...okay, okay. I won't touch anything."

Ilsa hung up the phone and found she was holding herself up with white knuckles gripped to her desk. She forced herself to look. A canvas stood upright on its end in a large puddle of blood. She floated towards it, surprised she even had the strength. She got closer to the canvas and stepped around Elliot's body.

"Oh, my God. How did you do this?" She looked to the back of the gallery and could see it was still locked. No alarms were set off. *How?*

She lifted the canvas and her eyes darted from the picture to the body.

"It's you. You crazy son of bitch. It's you in your own blood."

Then she had a very brilliant insight and the earth stopped.

"Huh. What are the chances that I would choose a real psycho? Elliot, your paintings will skyrocket after this. And at 20% commission…." Ilsa was positively ecstatic.

She leaned over Elliot's body, "Thank you, Liebling."

She heard the sirens and returned the blood-soaked canvas to the puddle.

"They're coming."

Ilsa surveyed the portraits on the wall with new admiration. She was drawn to Adelaide, the old woman's past a reminder of her own family sins. She noticed paint at the bottom edge of the canvas and ran the tip of her finger along it.

Sloppy artist, too.

But it wasn't paint. It was a fresh drop of blood. "How did blood get all the way to this end of the gallery?"

She smeared the blood between her finger and thumb, and then wiped it on her pant leg.

The paramedics were outside the door first. She gave her body a shake and prepared to be the grieving friend.

Ilsa turned. An unfamiliar tingle went up her neck. Then, she thought she heard whispering.

Imagination and Prognostication

Average Read Time: 8 min.

Gina Vasilescu sees things. She sees the future – the possible, impossible or probable. Her visions, real or imagined, are indistinguishable.

And therein lies the problem.

So when she saw her newlywed neighbor kill his wife, she wasn't sure if she should call 911 or finish making her grilled cheese sandwich.

Gina's visions started at the cusp of puberty when all things are awakened. That was fifteen years ago. She's had that many years to accommodate her life to the intrusions of sporadic images, random smells and possible future events that may or may not occur. Her mother had this gift, or curse, and guided her through these incidents which included something in between breathing exercises and ignoring that they ever

101

happened. Their gypsy-Romanian bloodline ensured that she, her mother and her grandmother all possessed the ability to see future events. Her great-grandmother was a traveling palm reader, like the kind in those old horror movies. Quite well-known in that part of Europe, Gina was told. Until they burned her for witchcraft. Then the family left Romania and refused to acknowledge any supernatural abilities. Fear gripped all their descendants. They were never to speak of it, never to reveal it, never to acknowledge it.

Gina, however, embraced it. She regarded it as a gift from God. *Why would God instill such a powerful blessing if she were to not use it?* Her mother and grandmother crossed themselves profusely whenever she started pontificating the virtues of prognostication. Although she considered it a blessing - however unreliable, however untenable to reality - she was careful to whom and when she would disclose her secret, lest she freak people out with premonitions of death, destruction or termination of employment. But she divulged her family secret to her boyfriend Joe before they moved into together. Full disclosure and all. He was casual about it, perhaps humoring her. "Well, that's cool." *No, not cool all the time.*

She got used to the visions, learned to interpret them, albeit not always with one hundred percent accuracy. When they did occur, they were frightening at first, these unbidden flashes of events, not always crystal clear like watching Netflix. Sometimes details were misinterpreted, and that made warnings sketchy at best. And it was difficult to distinguish if these things were actually happening as she saw them, if they were visions of things to come, or eccentric imagination.

That was another huge problem.

One most embarrassing incident happened when she was sixteen. At the time, they lived in Queens where the houses were so close together, if you sneezed your neighbor blessed you. An elderly couple lived next door - Mr. and Mrs. Tidwell. Gina saw Mrs. Tidwell chopping off Mr. Tidwell's arm on the kitchen butcher block. Mrs. Tidwell was slamming away with a giant meat cleaver and she could hear the bone crushing chops.

Whack! Whack!

Gina ran into the kitchen, her red hair flying around her head like a banshee, to stop the mutilation. Turned out Mr. Tidwell was holding still a rack of ribs for the bar-b-que that night. Mr. and Mrs. Tidwell actually lived to 98 and 102 years old, respectively. No chopping was involved with their passing. So Gina apologized for her psychotic episode and from then on refrained from barging into other people's house, accusing them of murder, without first having some kind of substantiating evidence.

Sometimes her visions were incredibly accurate. Last summer, she saw the neighbor's terrier run into the street and get hit by an ice cream truck. She saw it. She heard the bell. She heard the music and the dog barking. She laughed at the scene, "Who doesn't like ice cream?" But the dog didn't stop and neither did the truck and, splat. When she ran into the house to grab Joe and cried they had to get the neighbors, there was no truck and no dog.

A week later, Gina heard the bell, heard the music and the dog barking. And she knew. Joe didn't think it was so cool anymore. That was just too much of a coincidence for him so now when she says she sees something, they hold their breath. And wait. And like Vegas, they take odds whether it's imagination or prognostication. The uncertainty made her life always waiting for the unexpected. Like waiting for the other shoe to drop. Most people would think she were Sicilian. But she learned to accept the uncertainty. Modern pharmaceuticals helped, too.

So after weighing her options and pushing aside the shellshock from the incidents with the Tidwells and ice cream truck, Gina decided that she had to confirm that her neighbor, the new Mrs. Megan Harrington, was all right. She turned off the stove and slipped the sandwich onto a plate. She went to her room and pulled out an emerald green blouse she promised to Megan for an interview.

She took calming breaths and exited her house. Her heart was pounding so, she could barely hear the summer cicadas chirping or the sprinklers tapping. She approached their door and rang the bell. More calming breaths. Heavy footsteps stopped and she envisioned Michael Harrington peering through the peephole. He unlocked the door and it swung open, "Gina, hi."

"Hey, Michael. Is…Megan home?"

"Yeah, come in."

"She is?"

"Yeah. She's in the living room."

Sure she is. That's where I saw you strangling her.

Gina followed Michael into a very quiet house and chills ran up her back. In a moment of panic, she realized she didn't tell anyone where she was. She lagged behind. Michael swept his hand and said, "Baaack here," and smiled.

He can be so charming, can't he.

"Hey, Gina," said a very alive Megan.

Gina let out a sigh and relaxed. *Okay, one of my imagination things.*

"Hey, great color." Megan elbowed Gina, "Us gingers look awesome in green, don't we? Michael, don't we look great in green?"

Michael was hypnotized by the baseball game.

"Michael!"

"Yeah, great in green. Great in green."

"Don't mind him. He zones whenever a game is on…You okay, Gina? You look a little pale?"

"Yeah, you're going to laugh," and Gina forced a giggle. "You're all right, yeah?"

"I'm fine. Why?"

"Well, from my kitchen, I can see right into this room, the windows are so big. And I thought…you're going to think I'm nuts." And Gina dropped her voice into a whisper, "I thought I saw Michael…hurting you."

"Hurting me?"

Michael's head turned towards them and then back to the 50 inch screen.

"Well, I guess I was just...imagining things."

"That's a little out there, Gina. You see things often?"

Yeah, I do.

Megan rubbed Gina's arms as if warming them. "Newly married he still loves me, right Michael?" A grunt came from the Lazy-Boy chair. "Thanks for the shirt. I'll get it back to you right after my interview."

"Good luck with that." She started walking to the front hallway.

I have to get out of here.

Megan followed. "Thanks. Hey, Michael. Gina's leaving."

He lifted his beer high and said, "Later, Gina."

Gina left with the uneasy feeling that although this vision may not have happened today, it may happen. May. And that was unsettling.

Five days passed without an incident. She didn't mention anything to Joe because, lately, he was just weirded out with her woo-woo powers as he came to call them.

Megan had left a message on her answering machine and it said that she could come by any day after Thursday to get her shirt. Just look for her car in the driveway.

So on Friday, Gina saw her Mercedes parked in the Harrington driveway. She turned off General Hospital and ran over to the house, hoping it was early enough that Michael wouldn't be home. She rang the bell and didn't hear anyone approach until the door opened.

It was Michael. "Gina, hi. I bet you're here for your shirt."

"Hey. Is Megan here?"

"At work. Come in."

"But her car --,"

"Yeah, I borrowed it for the day. Mine's in for an oil change. Come in." And then Michael did the unthinkable. He broke the first rule of Good Neighbor Etiquette; he touched her. He reached out and took her wrist and guided her in. Gina was so caught off guard that she complied as if in a trance.

"She left the shirt in the other room," not letting go of Gina's wrist.

Goosebumps covered her body from the inside out. She felt the panic well up and build, and her blood was pounding in her ears. She didn't leave a note or text Joe where she was. Once again, no one knew where she was. *Idiot.*

"I can come back later, when Megan's home."

"Nonsense. I have it right here."

The walk through the house for Gina felt like it took forever and the sunshine blinded her when they entered the living room. Michael finally let go of her arm and grabbed the shirt wrapped in dry cleaner plastic. He held it out to Gina. Just as she reached for it, he pulled it back. "That was a weird story you told Megan the other day."

"Story?"

"You know, about me hurting her."

"I see things sometimes. I have a vivid imagination. People tell me I ought to write," and she forced a laugh.

He crumpled the shirt into a ball and tossed is aside. Michael didn't think she was so funny. "It was very unnerving what you…saw. Because what you saw was what I was thinking."

Michael walked around the room, always between Gina and the door. "Megan and I knew each other in high school. Her family was FREAKIN' wealthy. Me, not so much. So when we met up again at our ten year reunion, I asked her out. Then one thing led to another, you know how that goes. Her parents are gone. She's an only child. She got *everything*. And if she disappears, guess who gets the whole kit and caboodle?" He seemed almost giddy.

He studied Gina's kitchen window from his living room. "Wow, you would have had a perfect view. How stupid of me."

"I have no idea where you're going with this. I need to leave."

"Where am I going. Where am I going. I'm not going anywhere. Megan is. You were right. What are you, psychic? A witch? What?"

Gina didn't answer. Her eyes sprinted around the room looking for an escape. Before she knew it, Michael was on her, his beefy fingers wrapped around her neck.

"I can't…have…you telling anyone what you think you might have…seen."

And he squeezed.

She flailed her arms but couldn't get around his massive frame. She slammed her knee into his groin but missed and hit his thigh. He clamped his iron legs around her knees.

"How could you have known what I was thinking?" he said as he shook her.

Gina couldn't breathe anymore and the light in the room began to fade. *Joe doesn't know where I am.* Then in the flashes of residual light, she saw her vision again. It wasn't clear then, but it was now. It wasn't Megan in her vision. It was her. The red hair and fair skin was her, not Megan. And the vision faded as well.

And Joe doesn't know where I am. Joe doesn't know where I am.

Cup o' Joe

The Traveller

Average Read Time: 1 min 20 sec.

Galactic Date 12.5.2063

Midra Samuels appeared outside the geo-dome and read the atmosphere. "Samuels to IS Petraeus. Air breathable. Life forms unknown. Will investigate."

"Acknowledged, Ensign Samuels. Proceed with caution."

Midra had been on the Interstellar Ship Petraeus for six months, and had waited even longer for an assignment to explore a new planet, make contact, build relations.

She unsnapped her helmet and inhaled. She was greeted by a hint of lavender mixed with earthy soil, and the cells of her body seemed infused with a stillness. She studied the masterful construction of the geo-dome and scanned the area for inhabitants. A life form blipped forty meters ahead. She made her way through the trees which surrounded the geo-dome; they parted for her, as if welcoming her. Twenty inhabitants, registering as one being, formed a perfect circle. They extended their hands to Ensign Samuels to join them.

****

"Is her Excursion complete, Doctor?" asked Antona Samuels.

"Yup. She's fine." He noted, but dismissed the mother's constant blanket tucking.

"She can go on any Excursion as long as she's...like this."

"Absolutely. Patients have shown excellent recovery from a coma when we use Stimulated Brain Activity."

Relief washed over her and she stroked her daughter's forehead. "She had always wanted to attend Interstellar Academy. Where can she go next?"

The doctor swooped his hand like a magician over a box. "Wherever you think she'd like."

Antona Samuels wiped her nose with her sleeve. "I brought videos from home. You said you can upload them." She removed a mini-DVD from her bag. "I'd like her to come home."

The Caretaker

Average Read Time: 3 min. 15 sec.

She opened her white patent leather handbag with a snap, and if moths could flutter out and about, they would have. It had an ancient smell. A kind of combination of sticky cherry cough drops and dehydrated Wet Naps. But this bag had been her mother's and if it was good enough for her for fifty years, it was good enough for Francie.

"Pansies," she thought, "Yes, pansies would be nice this time. I'll take two packages of the purple pansies, Mike."

"Just got them in, Ms. Stattler. Usually you get the mums."

This time would be different.

"I like the way their little faces turn
to the sun. It looks like they're smiling
up to heaven."

Francie juggled the flowers, her garden tools and large beach bag and pointed her car towards the place she could drive to in her sleep.

The green space was peaceful but thunder rumbled just to the north. She placed the flat of pansies at her feet and cleared away the weeds. Then she unpacked her bag unaware that her ritual was as methodical as a priest at Sunday service. She spread out her picnic blanket and made sure the corners were even and flat. She laid out her sandwich, wine bottle and a bag of ripened strawberries. She remembered how her mother loved strawberries with just a bit of sugar sprinkled on them. She was such a good daughter.

And then she sat down and waited.

Francie leaned over and brushed the fresh grass clippings from the top of the headstone.

"That's better. I'm here again…It's Tuesday."

Francie waited as if something was supposed to happen. But nothing ever does. Most of the time. Her mother is as silent now as she was in life. No greeting. No kind words.

Silence.

"Nothing for me today?" She paused. "And why would today be any different?"

She broke the turkey sandwich in two and brushed the crumbs off the blanket.

As if she were sharing it. But she didn't eat. Not just yet.

"Hm. Not even an insult about my dress. The fit or the color? I even changed my hair style since last week."

Peter's gone.

"Oh, you are there. Yes. Peter is gone, isn't he….And it was your venomous treatment and constant acerbic, biting remarks that drove him away. You know that."

He left you because you are lazy and you wouldn't have made a good wife.

Francie smiled. "Ahh, yes," she said through a full mouth, "There she is. The mother I know. *You* drove Peter away. And David, your favorite son, was the smart one. He moved himself and his family far away."

My David.

Even in death she could hear the affection.

He left me.

"David left because you drove him away. So he could lead a somewhat normal life, a normal family."

117

After a pause, her voice was quiet. "And he didn't leave YOU. He was an adult and he made an adult decision. I was your casualty."

Silence.

Francie made the sign of the cross and mumbled a prayer over her sandwich and strawberries, chastising herself that she forgot before her first bite. She took a sip of her wine and dabbed her lips.

Francie sat for what seemed like a very long time. It always does.

But she didn't speak of the weather. She didn't give her mother an update of her nieces and nephew. She did none of those things. She didn't tell her how she maintained the house exactly as she would have remembered it.

As if a shrine.

Careful not to disturb last week's mums, she moved the earth to one side.

Preserving it.

And gently placed this week's sacrifice in its place.

With a calming resignation, Francie looked up at her mother's name.

118

"You see, Momma, I'm done here. You need to be at peace. And so do I."

You're leaving me, too.

"No, Momma, I'm moving on. As it should be. I've said all I needed to say these past ten years.

Whether you heard me or not is another story. David and I will take turns sending flowers on your birthday, and a Christmas blanket on the holiday."

Silence.

Francie finished planting the pansies and returned the earth.

She said her final prayer as she patted lovingly around the tender stems.

"I should have never expected what you were never able to give."

Silence.

She ate half her sandwich and dumped the strawberries in the dirt. She touched the napkin to her lips and commenced clearing up her picnic. She rolled the blanket with all its contents like a rucksack.

As she made her way to the car, she turned back towards the grave site.

119

It was silent.

As it should be.

With a freedom she had almost never known in her forty-five years, Francie drove away.

It was now deathly quiet and a spring rain began to fall.

The only sound the cemetery residents heard was the tapping of the drops on the patent leather bag left behind.

What's Left Behind

Average Read Time: 1 min.

The kettle worked itself up to a full whistle. He had forgotten he put the water on. The Nurse's Angel will pour the tea.

He bent down, all his weight on the walker beside him, and looped his fingers into the slippers at the foot of the armchair.

Her armchair.

He left the needlepoint. With it half done, he could imagine she was returning soon, only gone to make the cup of chamomile tea and cinnamon toast. The house always had the lingering aroma of cinnamon. His grandchildren said it was mothballs. What do they know.

A twinkle of sunlight on the mantle caught his eye. They shared that pair of CVS *spectacles*, as she called them, because they had equally poor eyesight. They took turns reading the clues to the New York Times crossword and writing in the answers, and then switching every other one. She complained his handwriting was illegible and fought him every time she had to hand over the glasses and newspaper.

When time together begins, no one ever considers when time together ends. And what's left behind.

He looked at the slippers hanging from his fingers and placed them on the floor in front of her chair. He pulled his chair closer and heaved his body into the well-worn cushions. He studied the silence. And he wondered how long. How long.

A Place to Rest

Average Read Time: 4 min.

Aunt Sarah is old as it is hot. And in southern Georgia, that's sayin' somethin'. She forever sits on that porch and rocks. And rocks and rocks, just fannin' herself. She bellows, "Boy! You mind me and come warsh for supper!" Then the wind kicks up and blows her away like summer dandelion fluff.

And she is gone until next time.

She always has on a white dress with faded yellow flowers all smudged with peach juice and flour. She watches me and Becky play in front and every once in a while you hear her laugh. And not just any laugh. One that starts deep down in her belly, full of joy like she was really lovin' whatever we're doin' while she waits her turn. And Aunt Sarah ain't really a relation. She was here a long time before I walked down the east road.

Peyton Junction is at the crossroads to nowhere special and I doubt you will find it on any map. There

123

are four roads that lead out, or in: one goes east to the ocean, one goes north to the bigger town where we sell our peaches and pies, and one goes south and there ain't nothin' much for a very long time except more hot. And as Aunt Sarah says, "Who needs more hot?" Then there's one that goes west towards the far country. You can see our farm on the left if you're so inclined to visit.

The roads are long, dry and dusty. They ain't paved yet. Very few cars come here anyways. I'd like to ride in one. Soon, maybe. Ridin' in the back of the wagon makes for a bumpy ride and Misty don't move so fast anymore. I don't wear my church shoes on Sunday if we're goin' into town afterward on account they just get ruined, and then I have to hear Old Aunt Sarah tell me once again how we ain't made of money and I ought to know better.

Mr. McNulty is in the general store playin' checkers – all by hisself. Doesn't he ever get tired of playin' checkers? He never says nothin' to me. Ever. And like Aunt Sarah, whoosh, Mr. McNulty is gone too. When they disappear like that, I say they Whisper Out. I made that up myself.

Over there, Big Joe is under the giant maple. They still call it The Hangin' Tree on account that was where slaves were hung but that ain't happened for a long time. If I look close enough, and I try not to, I can see the

124

marks from where Big Joe got whooped. But he just sits there with his head in his hands, staring at the ground. I think he's waiting, although I'm not sure what he's waiting for anymore. He had many a chance to leave but he never takes it. I tell him it's time.

Most of the residents in Peyton Junction are old. That is, until I came. Aunt Sarah greeted me and said, "I was waiting on you, boy. Finally, I get to rest."

I must have done good that I got chosen. What Aunt Sarah passed on to me weighs heavy, greetin' all them folks as they come into town. But as Aunt Sarah says, "You got the job of helpin' others reconcile, Jeremiah. And then they move on. That's a blessin', boy, and one you should be proud of."

Once we had other children in the schoolhouse besides me and Becky. The Pickney family left. See, they saw it and didn't believe. When I ask Aunt Sarah why they didn't take their chance, her answer is always the same, "Some folks see, Sugar, and don't believe. So they leave here thinkin' they'll find a different answer someplace else."

Becky and I saw them pass my farm on the way to the far country.

"Jeremiah, stop starin' at them."

125

"I'm watchin' 'cause I don't see why they gotta leave here. Peyton Junction is all right. It's a nice place to stay." And I looked at her. "Becky, it's a nice place to stay."

Becky was quiet while she thought about her answer. "Cripes, Jeremiah, why you gotta *study* everybody. Can't you just…be?"

"That's all we're doin' here. Bein'. Ain't you bored?"

"That's WHY we're here, J. Haven't you figured that much out yet?"

She was right, I suppose. Then Aunt Sarah was there rockin' away, fannin' herself, watchin' me and Becky argue.

Mr. McNulty is back playin' checkers again.

Big Joe looked up from his ruminations. He's squintin' and sees something. But with a pain on his face that always seems to haunt him, he looks away. Then what he saw was gone and so was his chance. Then he was gone too.

Mr. McNulty is gone. And Aunt Sarah.

Aunt Sarah said once that when I'm ready to move on, my light will be my own. Not like the others. And

I'll be here a while on account I'm awaiting on my ma and pa. Then I'll go, too. We'll Whisper Out together.

I turned to Becky and, like the others, I watch her mix into the scorched, westbound dust.

I take out my rag and wipe my sweat. I wait along the roads and welcome the newcomers.

Time Travel of the Necessary Variety

Average Read Time: 14 ½ min.

Jack Finney had prepared for this journey for years. He wasn't sure what else to call it. He researched time travel since he was fourteen. He read the scientific journals and not so scientific journals. Sometimes the fringe science seemed more believable than the nay-sayers of the left-brained world so he decided to believe the whack-a-doos.

Now, he was twenty-eight and a card-carrying member of the Whack-a-doo Society. So some would say. But he believed it. He believed that traveling through time was as easy as catching the 1 Train to Battery Park. And he believed 1917 still existed.

Here.

Now.

And it was time for a first attempt. Jack closed his family photo album. He touched his mother's youthful face in a faded 1970's picture. He'll go visit her tomorrow. "I promised you," he said.

The weather was just right on January 15th 2016. A blizzard was forecast to start around six that night and continue until the next morning. The city's mayor banned cars from the streets and planes were grounded. Both would be a distraction and could ultimately ruin his trip. But in January 1917, it was a sunny winter day with a temperature of 45 degrees and so the circumstances were perfect.

Jack needed stuff. So to prepare, he haunted every antique shop in the city and even costume shops in the village. He needed everything to be time period perfect. He located two suits, one muted brown and the other grey, created for or actually from 1917. The worsted wool overcoat was handsome and could even pass for a vintage revival. The money was another issue. That required lots of legwork and extensive research. He attended several coin shows and coin shops in the tri-state area, and swiped up thousands of dollars' worth of pre-World War One coin and paper money. A hefty financial investment but unequivocally necessary if he were to exist at all.

After researching locations that exist simultaneously in both times, Jack decided on Central Park. It was an obvious choice. During a snowstorm,

Central Park is a time capsule. It could be 2016, 1963 or 1917. It retains the shadows and souls of every era as if preserved in a faded scrapbook for future generations. Perhaps the architects and designers intended this, a bridge from the past to the present. One could get lost in other centuries and other worlds; a fantastical respite during a forty-five minute lunch hour.

The snow started to fall sooner than predicted and Jack waited until it was considered a white-out before he suited up and pulled on his coat. He adjusted and re-adjusted his collar, jacket, pants - all while referring to the pictures he downloaded from the New York Public Library collection. His friend Eben Daniels, curator at the Museum of the City of New York, said the NYPL had the most comprehensive collection and he was right. Jack found research through the archives was his favorite part of his preparation. Sometimes he felt if he stared at the photos long enough, the people in the street and the horse-drawn carriages would actually move. And he'd hear the horses, the women's voices and the men hailing a cabbie.

Soon he wouldn't have to imagine 1917. Soon, very soon, he would join them.

Jack lived in an apartment on 95th Street and Central Park West. His mother, Margaret, inherited it from her mother and father who purchased it in the

1950's. Jack claimed residence after a car accident killed his father two years ago. A year after that, his mother got sick and he moved her to an assisted living facility and, a month ago, to hospice. The decision to move into the apartment was quite convenient for his project and actually prophetic. Out his door and into 1917. He pushed through the glass door of his apartment building and the bitter cold snapped the air from his lungs. He made a left at Central Park West and headed north to the 100th Street park entrance. He crossed the threshold into this other world, and it was ethereal and beautiful. He felt like he stepped into his own personal snow globe all shaken up. He worked hard at keeping a grasp of his reality and time period.

Because of his extensive historical research and dry-runs, Jack was able to locate the Loch Walking Path along West Drive. The Loch had been a well-known feature since the 17th century and he marveled that Lenape Indians most likely watered their horses here. He followed it through the area known as the North Woods, one of the most secluded areas in the park, and it's said that this is a bit of the Adirondacks in the city's own backyard.

Jack crossed over West Drive without even looking for cars. Because there were none. He looked for landmarks he knew well and the first was the Pool Grotto, a water feature that's fed by a pipe. Totally man-made and Jack called it cheating. He continued and did not even hear his own footsteps. Sound is naturally absorbed with the snow and he pushed on his ears to make sure they were still working. He passed not even one person so far. He was the only crazy out in this storm.

Finally, becoming clearer as he got closer, was the Huddlestone Arch. He chose this location for two reasons: it was there in 1917 and it's still here looking exactly as it did then. The other reason is that Huddlestone Arch is one of the least known stone arches in the park and the chances of someone coming by in a blizzard are remote. Even though daily traffic crosses over it, no one really *sees* it. He planned this so well. He was quite impressed with himself. He couldn't fail.

The street lamps were a fuzzy glow through the snow but it was enough for him to see. He sat on a dilapidated wooden bench beside the ravine and he began. He breathed in and out, in and out, and then closed his eyes. He repeated to himself, "I'm in 1917. It's 1917."

The quiet of the shallow water was almost eerie. New York City is never quiet with Mother Earth's sounds. But even this quiet began to fade. He heard the virtually silent hooves of a horse drawn carriage which, if the current mayor had his way, may be a permanent addition to Eben's museum and an anthropological footnote in this city's history. And then the hooves faded, too.

After an unidentified amount of time, he tested not where but *when* he was by opening his eyes to little blurry slits. The lamplight still glowed but instead of a steady orb, it was a flickering glow – gaslight. He smiled, closed his eyes and continued to breathe and repeat, "1917. I'm in 1917." Jack had no idea how long he had been on that bench. It didn't matter; time stopped. Or it became irrelevant.

A calm washed over his body and he felt warmth on his face. He blinked his eyes until he adjusted to his surroundings. Nothing. He was still home.

"No, I couldn't be. There's no snow."

He swiveled his head left and right and saw the sun just setting. The gaslight of the streetlamps flickered. *Yes!*

He checked his antique pocket watch. Was it even correct? A gentleman with a fedora hat and a newspaper hiding his face walked past and Jack asked, "Excuse me, sir, can you tell me the time?"

The man slipped his hand in between the buttons of his coat and pulled out a watch, "It's…half past four."

"Thank you," said Jack. Perfect timing.

He exited on Central Park West, where he came in. Somehow it looked eerily similar. He flagged down a handsome cab by watching the man standing further down the street. When one finally stopped, he said, "Columbus Circle."

"Right, oh." And they were off.

He touched the cracked leather seat and swayed with the movement of the cab. He could smell a mix of horse and cold air, and he wondered if perhaps he were only dreaming.

At the circle, Jack paid the cabbie and gave him a generous tip. And there he waited. He knew what she looked like but there were so many people. And she would be coming from West 59th. She had lived – lives – in Hell's Kitchen.

He was surprised when he recognized her so easily. His heart was banging in his ears but he approached her tentatively so as not to frighten her. "Excuse me. Can you direct me to the Plaza Hotel?"

Her young smile was familiar and her eyes sparkled with the golden hour's light. "Why, I'm headed there myself. Just up this way. Follow me."

"Thank you. Do you mind if I walk with you? Or is that too forward?"

"Not at all. Are you visiting the city, sir?"

"You could say that. I'm John Finney. You can call me Jack."

"I'm Catherine McCallister. I work at the Plaza at night, at the Flower shop getting the arrangements ready for the next day. So you lucked out, Jack, when you stopped me."

"Indeed I did." He could see why anyone would fall in love with her immediately. She had an aura about her and, when she spoke, her voice had a cadence that was unlike twenty-first century women. But that part you couldn't get from a picture. Imagination takes over to fall in love from a picture.

The hotel was stunning at only ten years old and another place where it could be 2016 or 1917. "Could I see you again? Maybe tea here, tomorrow afternoon?"

"I would love that, Jack. I've worked here for four years and have never indulged in their afternoon tea." Then she leaned in. "We're not supposed to mingle, you know."

"Come disguised." And they both covered their laughs at their own secret.

135

So Jack met Catherine for tea the next day and the day after that. He became quite good at travelling back and forth in time. He was so adept that after one week, he took to transporting himself right in the lobby of The Plaza. He'd choose a quiet corner with vintage furnishing to make it easier. His large Irish nose would grab a hint of ancient cigar smoke that still lingered in the wood paneling, and he marveled at the period architectural details that have survived over a hundred years and through the pain-staking renovation in 2002.

He was sure it would work each and every time. Now, it was time he told Eben.

****

"Dude, that's a story," said Eben. He shuffled some papers on his desk and moved about his office at The Museum of the City of New York. He looked sideways at Jack's clothes and wondered if he was losing his mind. His mother and all.

"It's all true. I swear, Eben. You know how long I've been researching this topic."

"Years."

"*Years*."

"As long as I've known you." Eben wanted to believe him. Something like that would be everything he's worked for at the museum come to life. Like how the paleontologists felt when they got to Jurassic Park. "Where's the proof, Jack. How do I know you just didn't hypnotize yourself and dreamt it?"

Jack was quiet. He hadn't thought that Eben would be so hard to convince. Eben believed him when he told him about his night with Tempy Silverman in high school. He was very jealous. And he believed about the strange lights that hovered above his car on Riverside Drive the night of the black-out. (At least he *thought* Eben believed him).

Jack stood up. "I'll get you proof." And he knew exactly what he needed to do, too.

"Wait, don't leave with your pantyhose in a knot. Let's get lunch."

"I have a date for tea," and he left.

Theoretically, he could have had lunch with Eben and then tea with Catherine; time was at his will. His to manipulate. But he needed to prove to Eben he visited with a Catherine McCalllister in 1917. He needed to prove it very soon.

Because Eben's timetable was not malleable.

****

137

After Jack and Catherine met for tea on the eighth day, they took a walk. He knew the photography studio was a block and a half down on the same side of the street, so "happening to pass by" was quite in the realm of believability. Their conversation was easy and topics changed fluidly. Jack had to be careful not to reveal anything past 1917. Like Googling things can sound inappropriate. He also had to remind himself to keep this platonic.

Jack paused in front of Brady's Photography Studio on Fifth Avenue.

"Catherine, let's get our portrait taken together. I would love a keep-sake."

"Why, Jack, are you going somewhere?"

He took her arm and guided her into the studio, "Just…a reminder. For always."

Catherine agreed but only if she were to have one as well.

Deal.

After their sitting, they exited the studio each with a receipt identifying the session. The sun was setting and it reminded Jack of the first day he arrived. He wasn't sure he wanted to leave. He had nothing really to go back to. But he knew he couldn't stay here either. He didn't belong with Catherine or in 1917.

Jack kissed the back of her hand and said, "I have to go."

Catherine pouted. "Tomorrow then?"

"Tomorrow."

But Jack never came.

He did make one more trip four days later, at night, when he knew he wouldn't run into her, to pick up his portrait. His was waiting for him. Catherine's was gone. Of course.

Jack returned for the last time to 2016 and headed for Eben's office. His secretary said he was on the phone but he pushed through the door anyway and dropped the portrait on his desk.

"Let me call you back, Jim," and he hung up. Eben touched the picture to see if it was real because it was hard to believe what he was seeing. "This is from one of those old-timey shops, right?"

"Christ, Eben, I was there. Look at it. The paperboard. The stamp on the back. Brady's Photography Studio hasn't existed since 1939."

"This is Catherine?" He touched the outline of her face. "You met this woman? She actually exists? Like exists right now?"

"Yes. She was smart and funny and…beautiful. She had a quality about her that was so different from the women we meet here."

"Not like Tempy Silverman, I guess."

"Yeah, no."

They were both quiet as Eben stared at the picture.

Jack whispered, "Just think, Eben. You can go back. All of what you've devoted your life to, you can see it as it really happened, as it *happens*." He let that sink in.

"What did she sound like?"

"Her voice was sweet and she had an accent I can't put my finger on. Sort of like Katherine Hepburn, but not as snooty."

"Mid-Atlantic accent." Eben smiled and leaned back in his cushy chair and rocked. "So she was educated."

Jack was getting excited. "I can show you how."

Eben - without taking his eyes off the portrait - said, "Show me."

****

Jack never time travelled again. He righted the time line and that was his intent. Now his life was his own.

The next day, he visited his mother in the facility.

"Mom, I did it. I really did it."

Her weak lips formed a smile and she lifted her hand. He took it.

"I sent Eben back to 1917 to meet your great-great grandmother. I'm still here. You're still here. He must have met her right where I told him or else we wouldn't be here."

"Let me see the portrait," she whispered.

Jack opened the photo album and held the book up so she could see the portrait of her son and his distant grandmother. "Job well done, Jack."

His whole life was preparation for that day. He had to meet Eben and befriend him years before righting the timeline; it was a set-up for his family to even exist. But the thing was, Eben was his best friend and will miss him the rest of his life.

And if he thought about it, he would be dizzy. What really came first? Jack travelling back to 1917 and crossed paths with his own way-back grandmother, or Eben falling in love with Catherine through a picture? Was Jack his guide, in a sense, to travel in time to meet her? Did Jack make it possible for Eben to fall in love with her?

Jack slipped an old-timey photo of Catherine, and someone else very familiar, into the album. "I'll miss you, buddy."

Eben Daniels - who died in 1988, the year Jack was born - was Jack's own way-back grandfather.

Miss Agnes Tweedie
and Her Very Curious Bookshop

Average Read Time: 13 ½ min.

Miss Agnes Tweedie has been the caretaker of the bookshop always, although the shop has not always been noticed. Not by the residents of Greenwich Village, not by the tourists and not by the daily passerby's. That is, unless you're supposed to notice it.

Madeline Perry lived three blocks away. Three short blocks and she stood before the window reading it over and over, "Miss Tweedie's Bookshop. Books for all Occasions."

She looked around the block, and the other shops were as they were the day before.

What's missing that this is here now?

"I might as well take a look. Support the local economy," grateful for a little air conditioning break on the warm spring afternoon.

She passed through the glass door leaving the city noise behind and the bell tinkled alerting her presence. The sun shone through a warm dusty haze that cast muted tones over the interior of the shop – as if dipped in sepia and preserved in time. Madeline could see an older woman behind a worn wooden counter at the end of the narrow, book-filled shop.

The woman looked up at the bell, smiled, lifted a section of the counter and walked toward her. "Come. Come in, my dear. Welcome to my book shop. I'm Miss Tweedie. I'm the caretaker of this fine shop. I have a wide selection. I'm sure you'll find what you came for."

Her grey hair was pulled tight into a neat bun. She wore a ruffled shirt, a plaid skirt and sensible shoes. Her British accent was clear, distinct and refined but welcoming and warm.

"Well, I'm not really looking for anything in particular. Just looking."

Madeline checked the time on her phone. Not that she had any plans. At the edge of the counter by the door, as if to greet visitors, was a life-size cat statue.

Madeline approached it and stared into its crystal blue eyes. "This is beautiful. What kind of stone is it?"

"Horatio is made of obsidian. All the way from Egypt. Cats were regarded as sacred in Egypt, you know."

"I read that somewhere." Madeline moved into the shop. "I've never noticed this shop before."

"Perhaps that's because you've never needed to before."

Madeline shrugged. "Like I said, I'm not looking for anything."

"Of course, you are. That's why you're here. That's why everyone comes. The writings of the ages solve all problems. They guide you, encourage you, heal you. They exist for you, for you to return to over and over whenever you need them."

Miss Tweedie inhaled. "And don't you love the aroma, my dear? I do. I wish they made a candle called Ancient Library, then we could have this smell enfold us always. But the books latch themselves on to me and they come home with me. How lucky am I, right? To always have that surround me. Always. You will see. The bookshop will attach itself to you, too. You see, my books are here for you. For you and anyone else who needs them. And when you are done with a book, you return it for someone else to take."

"These books are not to purchase?"

"Oh my, no. It's like a…lending library. But these books are unique." She gazed with love at the dusty tomes. "You'll not find these anywhere else. You may find the author's works elsewhere but not these rare editions. That's what makes my shop so special. Among other things."

A black cat wound its body around Madeline's leg and she bent down to pet him. He had blue eyes. When she looked to the counter, the statue was gone. Miss Tweedie swatted her hand.

"Horatio, go 'way. Go find a mouse to chance or something."

"Is that…? Is he…?"

"What, my dear."

"Never mind," and Madeline shook off the weirdness and wandered past the shelves. "I'm really not in need of any book in particular. I don't read much anyway. I haven't the time. Work and all."

She looked over her shoulder several times at the black cat following the old woman up and down the store.

Miss Tweedie called out, "I always tend to decipher what my customers are here for. Do not fret. What do you do, by the way, my dear?"

"I'm a painter. I hand-paint furniture and signs. Things like that."

"How lovely. Good for the soul to bring beauty into the world."

Miss Tweedie scratched her chin in thought and scanned the massive but well-organized bookshelves. Then she approached a library ladder on wheels, stepped on the second rung and pushed off with her other foot, sending her flying down the rail. She ran her crooked finger along the spines then stopped and climbed down.

"Perhaps if I tell you about a couple of my past customers it will help us decide what you are looking for. Where should I start? Oh, I remember a darling young woman. So sad when she arrived. Have you a few minutes?"

Madeline nodded.

"Oh, good." Miss Tweedie pulled out a stool and gestured for her customer to sit. "It was 1920, just this time of year."

Madeline tilted her head. *1920. How old is this woman?*

"It was warm for spring but it's always a bit stuffy in the city, with the buildings and all with no breeze. Not like by the shore of Brighton where I'm from. I opened this shop here as I was supposed to and that's how I ended up here. Oh, look at me digressing. You're so patient with an old woman, my dear. God Bless you." She took a deep breath. "So this darling young woman entered my shop. You remind me of her, too…"

Jane McBride stood outside Miss Tweedie's Bookshop, adjusted her waistcoat and pulled at her gloves. Only after that, she turned the knob. A friend had suggested she stop in. "You'll find whatever you're looking for when you visit Miss Tweedie's. I know," her friend said. Jane wasn't really interested in browsing an unfamiliar bookshop. She liked Waldendorf's. But she was curious.

"Welcome, my dear child. Warm today, isn't it? Can I help you?"

Jane glanced around with one foot mentally out the door. "A friend suggested I stop in. I usually shop on the upper West Side but she spoke such high praises of your shop, I just had to come and see for myself."

"I'm so glad you did." Miss Tweedie seemed to study Jane. "Today is a special day, isn't it?"

Jane diverted her eyes and a sadness emanated from her in waves. "It is. I buried my husband two years ago today. He died in the war."

"I'm so sorry, my dear."

Miss Tweedie's cat appeared on the counter. She stroked the black fur. "It's said that animals have a sixth sense about these things. He's come to comfort you, haven't you Horatio?"

Jane scratched the cat behind its ears which led to a satisfied purr. "I thought perhaps a new book would be a good distraction. What can you suggest?"

Miss Tweedie took both her hands and gave them a squeeze. "I know. It's right here and it's one of my favorites." She shuffled to a slim, leather-bound book decorated with floral gold leafing.

Jane ran her hand over the title. "Hope Springs Eternal."

"Doesn't it, my dear."

"I'm not so sure it does." She flipped the pages and asked, "How much?"

"How much what?"

Jane snapped open her handbag, "How much for the book?"

"No, no. No charge, my dear. This is a borrowing bookshop."

"How do you stay open?"

"Oh, I get by, child." And as Miss Tweedie placed the book in brown paper and twine she said, "I want you to do something for me. Do you know the Shakespeare Garden in Central Park? On the West Side and 79th."

"I do."

"I want you to go there, bring the book, read through it between noon and two every day."

"Every day? Why?"

"Oh, wonderful things happen when you read my books. You will feel hope."

Hope. She liked the sound of that since her Well of Hope was just about dried up.

The next day, Jane found a shady spot next to the Spanish Lavender and settled in with her new book. From noon to two, she read. The next day, she sat among the lavender from noon to two and read. The day after that she returned to the garden, and started to wonder if Miss Tweedie was barmy or if she was.

"Excuse me."

Jane looked up and her breath stopped at the silhouetted man standing before her, a crown of sun's rays behind him. The broad shoulders, long arms and legs — her husband.

He stepped into the shade, "Oh, I'm terribly sorry. Didn't mean to frighten you."

It wasn't her husband. Of course not. She chided herself for being so foolish. "No, it's quite all right. It was just the sun."

"I walk here at lunchtime. No better way to spend a bit of afternoon. I've seen you here every day, reading, and I've wanted to approach you. I mean, I'm not a fiend or masher or anything of the sort. My name is Walter O'Hanlon. I work as a clerk for Merchant & Palin. I noticed your book. 'Hope Springs Eternal.' Did you get that from Miss Tweedie's Bookshop?"

"I did indeed. How did you know?"

"Oh, one of my favorites. A collection of poems and quotes." And he slid next to her on the bench.

'The soul should always stand ajar,
ready to welcome the ecstatic experience.' "

"That's Emily Dickinson. I just read that one."

"Can I read another one to you, uh...?"

"Jane. Jane McBride."

"Thank you...Jane McBride." And he opened the book and found a passage with ease.

"It was many and many a year ago,
In a kingdom by the sea,
That a maiden there lived whom you may know
By the name of Annabel Lee;
And this maiden she lived with no other thought
Than to love and be loved by me.' "

Miss Tweedie wiped a tear from the corner of her eye with a tissue from her sleeve.

"Jane's story always gives me warm bubblies inside. Six months later, I received the book by post and a wedding announcement for the future Mr. and Mrs. Walter O'Hanlon."

Madeline reached out for the tissue as Miss Tweedie re-gained her composure. She really was growing quite fond of Miss Tweedie in the short time she was here. Madeline found herself falling under the spell of this woman's natural charm and this place that was filled with echoes of times past.

Miss Tweedie said, "Have you a few more minutes?" Without waiting for an answer, "Good. I have another story. A man came in last Christmas Eve. No overcoat, which was strange enough since it was snowing, and he looked so lost. Like a little boy who wandered from his mother in Macy's. He was dressed in a smart tweed jacket and carried a present under one arm. But I noticed his shoes most of all. You can tell an awful lot about a person by their shoes. His were expensive, polished and looked like they'd never seen the streets of Greenwich Village."

Miss Tweedie paused long enough to get out a rag and rubbed the top of the ancient counter.

"Take my shoes, for instance," and she lifted her foot. "These shoes are as old as Noah, I'd think. They've been with me for miles and miles, helping people find what they need, here at the shop. Miles and miles." She seemed to drift away for a second.

Madeline saw a pair of worn shoes. Miss Tweedie saw something very different.

153

"Anyway, he wandered in last Christmas Eve…"

"What can I help you find, my dear?"

"I'm not sure. I wasn't even intending to stop in," and he brushed the snow from his shoulders.

"Well, that's my specialty. Figuring out why you're here. I'll know soon enough." Miss Tweedie took his hand, *"I'm Miss Tweedie and welcome to my shop."* He smiled but Miss Tweedie noted that it wasn't a deep smile. Not a smile down to the core of his soul. *"You may wander for as long as you need to. I'm always here."*

"Thank you."

Miss Tweedie watched him as he perused the shelves, not pulling any particular book. His search was as lost as he was. The present shifted from one arm to the other and finally he placed it on the counter. Horatio jumped up and rubbed its body on the corners.

The man took out his keys and twirled the ring on his finger, a habit left over from his lifeguard days. Miss Tweedie caught sight of a medallion spinning on his key ring.

"Is that a pirate's symbol on your key ring?"

"Oh, yeah. It is. I got this down in Florida at the Pirate Museum when I was a kid," and he walked over so she could get a better look.

"It's fabulous. It reminds me of my more wild days," and Miss Tweedie blushed.

The man laughed, "Did you run with Blackbeard's pirates?"

The joke eluded Miss Tweedie and she answered, "Oh my, not him."

He frowned.

Miss Tweedie patted the man's hand. "I know exactly why you're here," and she moved to the ladder, pushed it to the far end of the store and scurried up to the very top. She brushed off the dust and her gnarled fingers placed it in his hands. "Treasure Island, lad."

Leather flakes snapped and floated to the floor when he opened the cover. "This was my favorite book when I was little. I read it over and over."

"I think it's time you read it again," said Miss Tweedie.

He fanned the pages with his thumb. "I even had a copy just like this and I wrote my name in red crayon on the inside. My father had a fit." His fingers stopped and

155

he stared at three letters scrawled in red crayon. "How can this be?"

Miss Tweedie smiled and didn't answer.

"That's amazing. How much?"

"You have a kind face. Just return it when you're done."

"You're kidding, right?"

Miss Tweedie stayed silent and his smile shone from within. He took her hand in his this time. "Merry Christmas, Miss Agnes Tweedie."

"Merry Christmas, James." And Miss Tweedie winked. "Or shall I call you...Jim."

"And then I shooed the man out the door into the snow. Horatio meowed to tell me he left his gift on the counter and I ran to the door but he was already gone. Ha, that's how quickly I move, my dear."

"Wait. Miss Tweedie. How did you know his name was James?"

"Oh, he must have introduced himself I suppose at some point. Anyway, he came back a week later, you know, to return the book. He was in these rugged clothes and he had a...uh...one of those rucksacks on his back.

156

And his shoes. Gone were those awful grown-up loafers. He had on work boots that were in dire need of scuffing. He said to me,

'I forgot so many things. I know what I'm supposed to do now. Thank you.'

I said, 'You are very welcome, my dear. Adventure awaits. Now go be happy.'

And when he looked at me this time, his eyes twinkled. And when there is love in your eyes, your soul is happy."

Miss Tweedie polished and she pushed the cat as she moved down the counter.

Madeline was quiet and then she took a leap and asked, "Why am I here?"

Miss Tweedie took her hand. Madeline could feel the bones under the vellum-thin skin, soft as rose petals. "This didn't take long. I know exactly why you're here. Follow me."

This time Madeline felt tingly all over. It was her turn and something wonderful was about to happen for her, too.

Four days later, a package arrived at Miss Tweedie's Bookshop. She assumed it was some of her borrowed books. But it wasn't what she expected. There was a book inside but underneath it was a hand-painted plaque on beautifully carved wood. She ran her fingertips over the exquisite calligraphy. It read,

"Those who are happiest are those who do the most for others."

She rummaged in the paper and found the card,

"I understand now. With much love, Madeline Perry."

"Oh, Horatio. How grand that life holds surprises even for me."

She wiped the dust from a shelf's edge and leaned the plaque against a row of books. Miss Tweedie stepped back and admired her gift as Horatio meowed, jumped to the end of the counter and then froze just as the bell tinkled. Miss Tweedie's soul shone as she extended her petal soft hand to welcome her new customer.

The á la Mode on Everything

Shunned and Stunned – Finalist 2nd Place,
IndiesUnlimited Flash Fiction Contest –
July 2015

Expectations and Misunderstandings – Winner,
IndiesUnlimited Flash Fiction Contest –
August 2015

Here There Be Dinosaurs – Finalist 2nd Place,
IndiesUnlimited Flash Fiction Contest –
August 2015

Halloween 2.0 – A version of this story appeared on
the site Creepypasta.com –
October 2015

Any Day Above Ground – This story appeared on
the site Creepypasta.com –
March 2016

RB Frank was awarded the *Manhattanville College
Alumni Award for Publications in Education* for
Bite Size Reads. A companion book is now
available for use in the classroom.
Available on Amazon.
Bite Size Reads
The Classroom Companion:
Creative Ideas and Lessons

Credits

The Orchard

"Don't Sit Under the Apple Tree."
Written by Lew Brown & Charles Tobias, performed
by The Andrews Sisters.

Miss Agnes Tweedie and Her Very Curious Bookshop

"It was many and many a year ago…"
- 'Annabel Lee' by Edgar Allen Poe.

"Those who are happiest…"
- Booker T. Washington.

Time Travel of the Necessary Variety

This piece is an homage. The main character shares
his name with the author Jack Finney, who wrote the
time-travel classic *Time and Again*.
The character name Eben is borrowed from the 1945
movie *Portrait of Jenny*. Both are among my favorites
and musts for the genre fanatic.

Acknowledgements

This compilation would not exist if it were not for the phenomenal community support of internet writers. Many of the stories are a result of flash fiction and short story contests. Some were winners, some placed and some never saw the light of day until I decided to put this together.

Indies Unlimited provided fabulous prompts and the opportunity to get my work out there. Their resource of information is unparalleled; they have everything you would ever need to know about writing, publishing, marketing, whatever.

CreepyPasta.com is another great forum for everything creepy and I thank them for giving me the opportunity to post there as well.

Manhattanville College's *School of Education Magazine* first published my educational articles and that's when I got the bug. Thanks for the infection!

Special thanks to my family who read everything awful and helped make it better.

Lastly, I could not have sharpened my skills and gained the confidence to venture into this wild blue yonder without the guidance of writing workshop facilitator Melissa Rubin at the Bryant Library who volunteered her time for the past three years. Thank you.

About the Author

RB.Frank graduated from Manhattanville College with a degree in Elementary Education and earned a master's degree in Reading and Clinical Diagnosis from Hofstra University. She published several educational articles in peer reviewed journals and stories highlighted in *The á la Mode on Everything*. She has completed one Middle Grade novel and is working on a Young Adult novel, all while she put this short story collection together. *(Your line is, "That's amazing.")* And someday, she would like her writing to be described as the prodigal child of the recombinant DNA of Rod Serling and Stephen King. She has a husband, two daughters and two dog-kids, Charlie Biscuit and Linus.

You may contact her through her website: rbfrank.com
Instagram @writingoutloud
Twitter @writingoutloud2